SLAPSHOTS #1

The Stars from Mars

Gordon Korman

SLAPSHOTS #1

The Stars from Mars

Cover by
Greg Banning

Scholastic Canada Ltd.

Toronto New York London Auckland Sydney
Mexico City New Delhi Hong Kong Buenos Aires

Scholastic Canada Ltd.
604 King Street West, Toronto, Ontario M5V 1E1, Canada

Scholastic Inc.
557 Broadway, New York, NY 10012, USA

Scholastic Australia Pty Limited
PO Box 579, Gosford, NSW 2250, Australia

Scholastic New Zealand Limited
Private Bag 94407, Greenmount, Auckland, New Zealand

Scholastic Children's Books
Euston House, 24 Eversholt Street, London NW1 1DB, UK

Library and Archives Canada Cataloguing in Publication

Korman, Gordon
The stars from Mars / Gordon Korman.
(Slapshots ; #1)

ISBN 0-590-70619-5 (bound).—ISBN 0-439-93869-4 (pbk.)

I. Title. II. Series
PS8571.O78S77 2002   jC813'.54   C2002-904089-2

ISBN-10 0-439-93869-4 / ISBN-13 978-0-439-93869-3

6 5 4 3 2   Printed in Canada   07 08 09 10

For Lord Stanley;
Thanks for the cup.

Chapter 1

The Cinderella team.

There was no better story for a sports reporter. It didn't matter if you were with *Sports Illustrated* or the Waterloo Elementary School *Gazette*. Unfortunately, I wrote for the *Gazette*. Salary: zero. But I knew that one day I would be working for a top magazine, or even covering sports on TV. All it took was hard work — and a little bit of luck.

The luck part was mostly finding something to write about: a great athlete, a turnaround season, a come-from-behind coach, or, best of all, a true underdog team.

It's hard. Some reporters never get their big chance. But I woke up one morning to find the ultimate underdogs practically sitting in my lap.

I had just given up jawbreakers, so I was in a lousy

mood — until I heard the news. A baboon couldn't miss it. Everyone on the school bus was psyched and screaming. I'm amazed the driver didn't swerve into the ditch.

After years of trying, our town was finally getting a hockey team in the Waterloo Slapshot League. You see, we went to Waterloo Elementary School; we used their police department and power company and public library. But we didn't actually live in the city. Our neighborhood was across a small canal in a town called Mars. No Martian jokes, please. We've heard them all — especially from the Waterloo kids at school.

"A team for Mars?" I asked skeptically. "Are you sure?"

I was cranky and twitchy. Man, was I missing my usual after-breakfast Licorice Cannonball. I could see my reflection in the bus's dirty window. It didn't even look like me without the telltale bulge in my cheek. Would everyone still call me Chipmunk now that I was off jawbreakers? I hate my real name — Clarence.

"My dad was at the big meeting," confirmed Jared Enoch. "He heard it with his own ears. Some of the league people voted against it. But the proposal still passed. We're in."

There was a rousing cheer from every throat on

the bus. We Marsers felt like second-class citizens in Waterloo.

"They've been keeping us out forever," mused Josh Colwin. "I wonder what made them change their minds."

"Are you kidding?" Jared crowed. "How could they say no? The guy who's going to coach us is a retired NHL player! None of the Waterloo teams have *that*!"

Josh sat forward in his seat. "A real old-time hockey player? Here in Mars?"

I pulled out my reporter's notebook. I never go anywhere without it. Who knows when something big is going to come up? And this sounded like it was going to be *huge*.

"Who is it?" I asked breathlessly. "Gordie Howe? Bobby Orr?"

Jared spread his arms in a grand gesture, like he was announcing the winner of the Nobel Prize. "The one and only Boom Boom Bolitsky!"

With my pencil frozen above the paper, I guess I forgot the dentist had me off jawbreakers. I bit down on a hard candy that wasn't there. My back teeth clacked together like the jaws of a bear trap. I'm amazed I didn't blow my ears off.

"Ow!"

There was laughter all around the bus.

", seriously," persisted Josh. He was a pretty ockey nut. "Who's Boom Boom Bolitsky?"

Jared shrugged. "I haven't heard of him either. But he was definitely in the NHL way back in the 1970s. Man, we've got it all."

"We've got zip," came the soft but firm voice of Alexia Colwin, Josh's twin sister.

Silence. All attention turned to Alexia. She operated on a kind of reverse volume control. When she had something important to say, she became very quiet. And when she was talking about hockey, we all listened. Alexia was the best player in Mars.

"*Think!*" she told us in her regular voice. "They don't want us. I heard there was a lot of yelling and screaming at that meeting when they took the vote. And that's just the adults. Think about how the Waterloo *kids* feel. Why should we sign up to be the league joke, so they can have a grand old time laughing at us, calling us Martians and space hicks and nebula nerds?"

"Nebula nerds," giggled Cal Torelli. "I get it. That's funny!" That guy could laugh reading a stop sign.

Josh bonked him on the head with his backpack.

"So you guys can volunteer to be insulted," Alexia went on. "But count me out."

Jared cleared his throat carefully. "Actually, I'm

kind of relieved to hear you say that, Lex. Waterloo Slapshot League is boys only."

We all held our breath. Alexia wasn't going to like that.

The bus groaned around a corner, springs and shocks protesting. I longed for the comfort of a lemon sourball.

When Alexia spoke again, her voice was so low that only the few of us right next to her heard what she said: "I'll see you at practice this afternoon."

"But —" My reporter's instinct urged me to keep the story moving. "This means you're going to break the boys-only rule?"

"Rules like that are against the law," Alexia insisted. "Waterloo Slapshot League is boys only because no girls have ever signed up — until now."

I put a star in the margin. I'd better keep an eye on Alexia. Maybe the league couldn't keep her out. But they sure weren't going to like letting her in.

The bus pulled into the school parking lot. Mrs. Kolodny, our driver, went into her daily unfunny joke. "We are now entering Earth's atmosphere," she called jovially. "Prepare for docking at Spaceport Waterloo."

Cal slapped his knee. "Spaceport Waterloo!" he guffawed. "Is that hilarious, or is it just me?"

"It's just you," Alexia assured him.

I scanned the playground. "I wonder if the news is out yet."

At that very moment, a large overripe beefsteak tomato exploded like a grenade against the windshield of the bus.

"I guess the news is out," said Alexia mildly.

Mrs. Kolodny turned on the wipers, smearing orange slime everywhere.

"Wait a minute." Frowning, Josh did a quick count of the hockey players on the bus. "Even with Lex, we've only got nine skaters."

Cal reached over and slapped me on the shoulder. "Chipmunk, you've got to sign up."

"Not me," I said instantly. I'm not athletically inclined. Okay, I stink. I mean, I am the yardstick by which all future stinking will be measured. But that's not why I said no. Just think of every locker room interview you've ever seen on TV. The athletes are always sweaty and bruised and limping and bleeding. And there's the reporter: dashing, cool, not a hair out of place. He jots down a few notes before going out to a first-class dinner, and then on to the airport to fly to his next city, and his next great game. You can keep the thrill of center ice, half-court, home plate, the end zone. I'll take a seat in the press box any day!

Josh was distraught. "But how are we going to do line changes if we don't even have two full lines?"

Jared snapped his fingers. "I forgot to tell you. The league's giving us one extra player, so we've got ten — some guy who didn't get his registration in on time."

"I pity that poor kid, let me tell you." Alexia grinned. "He's about to find out how it feels to be a Martian!"

I wrote it down, word for word. Alexia gave great quotes.

Chapter 2

I stayed after school to work on my story. While I was in the library, I did a little research on Boom Boom Bolitsky, the guy who was going to coach the new team of Marsers.

Put it this way: Boom Boom definitely played in the NHL, but that's about it. He got traded every three months — that's when he wasn't getting sent down to the minors. He must have been benched most of the time because he only had nine goals in a sixteen-year career. In other words, he was good enough to make it to the NHL. But out of all the pros, he must have been the crummiest.

I sort of felt bad for Josh and Jared and all the other players who thought they were going to be coached by an old-time hockey legend. But for me it was great. I mean, *underdog* was my whole story angle. And Boom Boom Bolitsky was so *under* that he needed an elevator to get up to the subbasement.

To get the opinion of the Waterloo players, I decided to drop in on the practice over at the community center. I was in luck. The team on the ice was none other than the Powerhouse Penguins, sponsored by Powerhouse Gas and Electric. They were last year's champions.

Captain Trent Ruben had the puck. I stopped making notes. When a guy like Trent starts stickhandling, you've got to give him your full attention.

Zoom!

He faked left and skated right, leaving the dazed defenseman spinning in circles. But as the star center of the HOT line roared in on the goalie, my reporter's sense started to tingle again. There was a flurry of activity around Coach Monahan. The players were going nuts. Outraged cries rang through the arena. Something was up.

With a flick of the wrist, the league's leading scorer popped the puck just over the goalie's catching glove. Trent raised his stick. I clapped.

We were the only ones celebrating.

You could tell Trent was used to a lot of high fives and congratulations, even in practice. When he didn't get any, he looked around to find out why. Man, the Penguins looked upset.

Trent must have thought so too. He called, "Hey, who died?"

"You did," moaned Happer Feldman. He was the *H* in the HOT line — *H*apper, *O*liver, and *T*rent.

"Will somebody please tell me what's going on!" Trent said impatiently.

I got out my notebook.

"Ruben." Coach Monahan put a sympathetic arm around Trent's shoulder pads. "There's a problem. Your registration form arrived late, and the rules say you have to give up your spot on the Penguins."

Trent stared in horror. "I'm out of the league?"

Talk about drama! He sounded like someone was pulling his tongue out through his left ear.

"Take it easy," soothed the coach. "You can still play. But you have to fill the next available space. That's on the newest team."

Happer was horrified. "But the newest team is the *Martians*!"

My jaw dropped. This news was so big that I didn't even get mad at that jerk Happer for calling us Martians. This was *Sports Illustrated* stuff!

"The Martians shouldn't even be *in* our league," insisted Oliver Witt, their third linemate, "and now they're going to have *Trent*? What about the HOT line?"

"I'm moving Gavin Avery over from the second unit," the coach told them.

"Happer, Oliver, and Gavin —" mused Happer. His eyes bulged. "The *HOG* line?! Coach, no!"

"Oh, poor you," snarled Trent. "I'm kicked off the team and all you care about is finding another center whose name starts with *T*!"

"Yeah, Happer!" added Oliver. "This is all your fault anyway! Your uncle is the president of the league. How could you let him do this to us?"

"You think he just phoned up and asked if I wanted to be on the HOG line, and I said sure?" cried Happer, banging his stick on the ice.

"Mr. Feldman can't help us," Monahan told them. "How would it look if he threw out the rule book and made an exception for his nephew's team?" He sighed. "Guys, as much as this stinks, it's part of hockey. Even NHL players get traded."

"Yeah, maybe," Trent told his ex-coach. "But how many of them get traded to Mars?"

Head spinning, I ran out of the community center. This wasn't just big, it was gigantic! I had information that nobody else knew! It was a scoop!

The agony of being only a kid closed in on me. I mean, if I worked for ESPN, I could go on TV and scoop the competition right out of their jockstraps!

But the Waterloo Elementary School *Gazette* only comes out once a month. The next paper was *three and a half weeks away*! By then my scoop would be as old as last Wednesday's meat loaf.

I set my jaw. Well, maybe I couldn't scoop the story in the *Gazette.* But at least I could be the first person to tell the team in Mars that they had the great Trent Ruben to look forward to.

I'd missed the school bus, but Waterloo Transit went to Mars every hour. What luck! I ran like a maniac, and just made the bus with two seconds to spare. Now I could catch the Mars team's first practice and break the news.

We were just rattling over the bridge when the car passed us. In it sat Trent Ruben and his mom. She was giving him a lift to Mars to practice with his new team.

"Doesn't this bus go any faster?" I howled in frustration.

The driver glared at me in the rearview mirror.

Chipmunk Adelman had a scoop, but no one would ever know.

Oh, how I longed for my usual after-school Volcano-Hot Cinnamon Lava-Ball!

| | | | | | Chapter 3

The Mars ice rink wasn't very much like the fancy community center in Waterloo. Except for a warm-up shack with a potbellied stove, it was completely outdoors. The nets were the portable aluminum kind, so you had to be really careful not to trip over the bricks that held them in place.

The ice surface was bumpy and uneven. When the weather was warm, a half-inch layer of slush formed over everything. If you fell, you were drenched.

I leaned against the boards with my notebook open and ready. I didn't want to miss Trent's reaction to his new team.

Only there *was* no reaction. He was in his own little world, shifting his weight from one skate to the other and scowling at anyone who dared to approach.

By contrast, Coach Boom Boom Bolitsky seemed gloriously happy to be there. Inside, I was beating myself up for not bringing a camera. Because no one would believe me if I tried to describe him.

Boom Boom was about fifty. He kind of reminded me of a praying mantis, since his posture was bent over and his eyes were wild and staring. He was balding in front, but had frizzy shoulder-length hair tied in a ponytail in the back. His long nose seemed to bend first left and then right. His beaming smile revealed three missing teeth.

"He's a hockey player, all right," whispered Alexia. "Look at that nose. I'll bet it's been broken three times."

"Coach?" piped up Josh, his voice muffled behind his goalie mask. "What NHL team did you used to play for?"

Boom Boom brightened. "Well, I was drafted by Detroit —"

I made a quick note: *Former Red Wing . . .*

"But they traded me to Boston, who shipped me off to L.A. Then I got sent down to the minors, and when I got the next call-up, it was from Toronto."

I was getting writer's cramp trying to take all this down. But the coach wasn't done yet.

"From there I went to Vancouver, New York, to Pittsburgh, and then on to Philly." He frowned. "I know I left something out, because I'm pretty sure I was a Black Hawk in there somewhere, since I met my wife in Chicago. Or was it St. Louis? Oh, well, that's what you get for playing sixteen years without a thingamajig."

The point on my pencil broke. Thingamajig?

The team just stared at him.

"Thingamajig?" Alexia queried.

"Thingamajig!" he insisted. "You know, one of those doohickeys! This!" He turned to the nearest player, Brian Azevedo, and pointed to his protective headgear.

"You mean a helmet?" asked Josh.

"Exactly." The coach beamed. "Now, the first order of business is to hand out the whatchamacallits."

"Whatchamacallits?" chorused half a dozen voices.

We weren't in suspense for long. Boom Boom reached into a large box and pulled out a hockey sweater. Against a green background, white letters proclaimed:

MARS HEALTH FOOD
Stars

Josh stared at the jersey in reverence. "We're the Stars."

I know a headline when I see it: *The Stars from Mars*. It had *Sports Illustrated* cover story written all over it! What a great name!

There was a stampede for the box. Heads disappeared inside green sweaters. You could tell this was a big moment for everybody.

Josh put it into words. "We knew we were joining the league, but this makes it official."

Coach Bolitsky blew his whistle. "You look beautiful!" he declared emotionally. "Now, we'll start off with some basic thingamabobs."

Didn't the coach know any nouns?

Jared took a stab at it. "Drills?"

Reporting on a practice with Coach Bolitsky was almost like being a translator. It was a real challenge to figure out what he was trying to say. And if it was rough for me, pity the poor players. They were scrambling around, sweating and struggling to understand Boom Boom's bellowed instructions.

"Put your whatsit on the whosis!" *Keep your stick on the ice.*

"Play the heejazz, not the dingus!" *Check the skater, not the puck.*

"The thing! Get the thing!" *The rebound! Cover the rebound!*

You had to feel sorry for Trent Ruben. The guy had just gone from MVP to the Twilight Zone. The best skater in the league took one stride, hit a bump, and fell flat on his face. This happened *five times* before he got the hang of the pebbly ice of the Mars rink.

I couldn't believe it. The same kid who was awesome at the community center an hour ago looked like a four-year-old who was just learning to skate. He was easily the worst player there.

He sucked it up for a while, struggling bravely. But when Coach Bolitsky took him aside and offered skating lessons, last year's leading scorer went a little ballistic.

"Skating lessons?!" he howled into the frigid late afternoon air. "I know how to skate, Coach! It's this rink! It's like the surface of — of *Mars*! You know — the planet, not the town."

Boom Boom laughed. "Hey, you've got to take the rough with the smooth. The good with the bad, the dingus with the doohickey." And he moved off to work with the defensemen.

Alexia swooped by on her white skates, splashing slush on Trent. Out of a whole town of people who didn't much like Mars jokes, she was the touchiest.

"Hey, hotshot, I thought you could skate."

Trent stared at her. "A *girl*?"

"Oh, you're a genius, too, not just a conceited jerk!" Alexia could be a pit bull when you pushed her buttons.

Huge in his goalie pads, Josh hurried over. "Back off, Lex." To Trent he said, "You know, we grew up on this ice. You'll get used to it too."

But Trent was still bug-eyed over Alexia. "She can't be on the team!"

"Trust me." Josh grinned. "Godzilla couldn't tell Lex what she can and can't do."

But later, during the bodychecking drill, Trent pulled up instead of putting his shoulder into Alexia. Enraged at the special treatment, she threw out a hip and sent him flying into the boards. I don't think the great Trent Ruben took a hit that hard all last season.

Boom Boom loved it. "Great!" he approved. "That's a perfect example of a thingamawhosis!"

He probably meant hip check.

I tried to analyze the team using my sportswriter's instincts. It was hard to say whether they were good or not. Certainly, nobody was zooming around like the Penguins had been at the community center. But not even Trent — the best Penguin — could zoom at this rink. So that didn't mean anything.

Brian Azevedo was our fastest skater going forward. But backward, he couldn't skate at all. Kyle Ickes, on the other hand, cruised backward like a Hall-of-Famer. But going forward, he could trip over the blue line. So Boom Boom put them together as a defense pair, which made a kind of weird sense. It proved that the coach knew more about hockey than he knew about English.

Boom Boom was a truly nice guy. He spent half an hour explaining the offside rule to Cal. And he never got mad when good old Cal went offside on the very next play. And he was always patient with big-mouthed Jared, who was convinced that the most important hockey skill was the penalty shot and practicing anything else was a waste of time.

"Penalty shot?" the coach repeated in amazement. "That's the rarest thingamajig in hockey! I played sixteen years, and I never took one! I was never even in a game with one!"

"But we have to be ready!" wheedled Jared. "Otherwise we'll be giving up a sure goal!"

"Later," promised Coach Bolitsky.

I made a note of it. Later meant never in a million years.

After practice, the coach invited the team, and me, too, back to his health food store for some whatchamacallits.

Trent was the only one who said no thanks. "My mom's waiting in the parking lot."

"Bring her along," Boom Boom invited.

"Well, I think she might be allergic to — uh — whatchamacallits," said Trent with a feeble smile.

It was pretty obvious that all he wanted to do was get out of Mars. You could hardly blame the guy. He was soaked to the skin from falling in the slush and battered from Alexia's body checks.

"Wimp!" mumbled Alexia. "Who needs him?"

Whatchamacallits turned out to be hot chocolates at Mars Health Food, which the coach ran with his wife.

Ah, Mrs. Bolitsky. My note-making pencil snapped in my hand when she came out of the kitchen with the tray. Josh started coughing like mad and had to be pounded on the back by his sister. Jared tripped over his chair and landed on his head on the floor.

Put it this way: Mrs. Bolitsky was the most beautiful, gorgeous, stunning, and totally awesome lady in the world. Compared to her, supermodels look like grizzly bears. She was six feet tall, with long black hair and eyes that just — forget it! I'm a sportswriter, not a poet.

We looked at Boom Boom — a really terrific guy, but come on! The Bolitskys were like Beauty and the Beast.

Alexia was completely disgusted with us. She was the one who broke the breathless silence.

"Great hot chocolate, Mrs. Bolitsky. Thanks."

"Oh, it's not hot chocolate, dear." She had a perfect voice that matched the rest of her. "It's made of carob gum. And the whipped cream is really a tofu product."

My throat closed up. It still tasted pretty good. But just knowing that all those gross things were in there kind of spoiled it. The coach was right the first time. We were drinking whatchamacallits.

I noticed an empty space in my check — just about the size of my usual predinner Tutti-Frutti Tooth-Crusher Glow-Ball.

Chapter 4 〔〔〔〔〔

The Mars Health Food Stars were scheduled to play their first game on Saturday at the Waterloo community center. When Coach Bolitsky found out I was writing about the Stars for the *Gazette*, he invited me to ride on the team bus.

It wasn't a real bus. It was actually the rusted old delivery truck for the health food store. So there were no seats. We all bounced around like Ping-Pong balls — which isn't fun when you're the only person not wearing heavy hockey pads. I got bonked over the head by Josh's goalie stick, and Cal thought it was so funny that he almost rolled out the double doors.

That wasn't all. Yesterday the coach had spilled an entire two-gallon container of garlic fish chowder with double cabbage in that truck. Even after a hose-down, everything reeked. And by the time we unloaded all the gear at the arena, we did too.

The outsiders from Mars took a few boos and cat-calls from the crowd in the lobby of the community center. Don't forget we were still the team that very few people wanted in the league.

"You guys stink!" howled a player from one of the other teams.

"Psst!" hissed Jared. "Does he mean stink like lousy at hockey, or stink like smell bad?"

"Keep walking," muttered Alexia. Her voice was so low it was barely a whisper.

The players had suited up at home, so all they had to do in the locker room was put on their skates.

"Our opponents are the Waffle Heaven Hurri-canes," announced Coach Bolitsky. "They finished dead last in the thingie the past two years. So they're not exactly champions. But remember — they've played together and we haven't. So we shouldn't get overconfident."

Overconfident? Didn't he see how scared the play-ers looked? I was writing like crazy because these are the details that make sports stories come alive. Josh was quadruple- and quintuple-knotting his goalie skates. Cal was banging the back of his head against the wall. The echo of helmet on cement was driving everybody crazy. Jared had his fingers jammed in between the bars of his face mask and was biting his nails. Even Alexia, who couldn't be frightened by a charging rhino, looked very pale and serious.

It was a really tense situation. As for me — well, the old Chipmunk would have been popping jawbreakers like peanuts. But now all I had to chew on was my pencil.

Josh looked at the clock on the wall. Three minutes to game time. He said what was on everybody's mind: "Where's Trent? He was supposed to meet us here."

"What did I tell you guys?" Alexia snorted in disgust. "The rats always desert the sinking ship."

"There's got to be an explanation," insisted Jared.

"Oh, there's an explanation, all right," Alexia raged. "He'd rather not play than be seen on the ice with us Martians! Good riddance, I say."

"Enough of this negative thingamabob," Coach Bolitsky interrupted firmly. "It's time to get out on the whatsit."

My pencil was just a blur. This was definitely *Sports Illustrated* material — the Stars from Mars, heading bravely out to play their first-ever game, insulted and abandoned by their only Waterloo teammate.

They filed out behind their coach and stopped

dead. For there, skating a warm-up by himself, was Trent Ruben. All the players except Alexia mobbed him, slapping him on the back and shoulders. It sort of looked like they'd already won the championship, even though the season hadn't started yet. I'm pretty sure the Hurricanes thought they were nuts. Trent just looked miserable.

The Hurricanes had a few fans in the arena, mostly parents and a handful of players from the early and late games of the day. But for our side, it seemed like half of Mars had shown up. So the Stars got a standing ovation for skating their warm-up. I hate to say it, but that turned out to be the high point of their day.

I guess I should have expected the Stars to be terrible. After all, they were brand-new at this business of being in a league. Sure, they'd played hockey — little pickup shinny games. But here there were rules, and refs, and face-offs, and a time clock. And here the stands were full of people. It was scary.

For starters, the Stars were used to the lumpy ice in Mars. This ice was as smooth as a tabletop, and freshly surfaced by a real Zamboni. Every single one of the Marsers had their feet slide out from under them. It looked like a battlefield after the war, with bodies all over the place.

Looking humiliated, Trent went from teammate to teammate, hauling them upright.

"I can make it on my own," said Alexia through clenched teeth.

Trent shrugged. "Suit yourself." And he left her there, struggling.

Hockey players hear cheers and boos, but it's not often that they get laughed at, even by their own parents. It was a really lousy beginning, and it had to hurt.

The only good news was that Trent was back to himself now that he was on familiar ice. He won the opening face-off, faked out the opposing center, and made the most beautiful pass I've ever seen. It was so perfect that Jared didn't even have to move his stick to get it as he streaked down the left wing.

"He's got a whatchamacallit!" brayed Boom Boom.

"A *hot chocolate*?" cried Cal, who must have been remembering last week's practice.

I was sitting in the front row, right behind the bench. "A breakaway!" I yowled. "A clean breakaway! Go, Jared!"

Caught behind the play, the Hurricanes' defenseman made a desperation move. He dove for the puck, but his outstretched stick got tangled up in Jared's skates instead. Down went Jared, and up went the referee's arm to signal a penalty.

The defenseman headed for the penalty box, but the referee called him back.

"Number ten was tripped with a clear path to the net," ruled the official. "That's a penalty shot."

Jared whipped his head around so fast that I'm amazed he didn't snap it off at the neck. "You see?" he howled at Coach Bolitsky. "A penalty shot! You said it hardly ever happens!"

Boom Boom called him over for instructions. "Okay, Jared, don't get nervous."

"I wouldn't have to be nervous if we'd done it in practice!" Jared complained.

"Listen," said the coach. "When you pick up the doojig, cruise in on the whatsit, and give a little whoopsy-doodle before you shoot."

Well, that was as clear as a brick wall. Jared just stared back, his eyes getting bigger and bigger. By the time the whistle blew, he was shaking with excitement. He couldn't even speak. We all wished him luck, and he made a sound like a car motor on a very cold morning.

The puck was placed at center ice. Jared skated up on it, reached out his stick, and missed. He whizzed right by, puckless.

"Go again." The referee grinned.

The stands tittered with laughter.

Jared made a U-turn, and this time he did pick up the puck. It's hard to describe what happened next, except to say that he fell apart. And I mean *really* fell apart! The puck rolled away from him, and his stick and one glove went with it. His skate lace came undone, and he tripped over it and went down in a heap. His helmet popped off and clattered into the face-off circle, face guard flapping. The second glove just got left behind as he slid on his backside toward the net. The goalie had to make the save — not on the puck, but on Jared. I'm sure there's never been anything like it in *Sports Illustrated*.

The stands rocked with merriment. It took all the Stars, and some of the Hurricanes, too, to get Jared's stuff back to the bench so he could get dressed again.

"I told you we should have practiced it!" Jared exclaimed righteously.

Like there was a drill for not coming unglued during a penalty shot.

Boom Boom was too nice to laugh along with everybody else. "Next practice," he promised.

If the Hurricanes had been the worst team in the league, they definitely no longer were. They led 4–0 by the end of the first period, and 9–0 by the end of the second. Our poor Josh was making a lot of saves, but missing a lot too. He wasn't getting much help from the defense. It always seemed like Kyle was the one who needed to go forward to make the play, and Brian was backing up. The other way around, they would have been great. This way, they usually ended up flat on the ice with two, or even three Hurricanes roaring in on Josh unchallenged. That's how they got nine goals. A good team would have had fifty.

Except for Trent, none of the Stars had ever played with line changes before. So there were eleven penalties for too many men on the ice. That meant the Stars were constantly shorthanded by a skater or two. Then there was the time that the first line came to the bench, and the second forgot to replace them. The result was the first five-on-zero rush in the history of hockey. Josh looked kind of lost, surrounded by so many purple shirts.

In the end, it really didn't matter how many players we had out there. They all fell down. Only Trent was on his feet. But a few of the others were starting to get the hang of it. Of course, the better Cal skated, the more he went offside. The guy just couldn't seem to figure out that the puck had to cross the blue line before he did.

The third period cranked up the pain level. When

it got to be 12–0, I crossed out my hopeful headline, *Miracle Comeback*, and replaced it with *Slaughter on Ice.*

"Go back to Mars!" came a cry from the Hurricanes' bench.

"How do you like the league so far, you cosmic hayseeds?"

"Go milk a meteor!"

"Milk a meteor!" laughed Cal, shaking his head. "Like meteors could give milk!"

"They're insulting us, you bonehead!" Alexia's face was a thundercloud behind a visor that was steaming up. "They won't get away with this," she said very softly.

"Now, now," Coach Bolitsky jumped in. "Sticks and stones may break my bones, but thingamajigs will never hurt me."

But Jared just couldn't keep his mouth shut. "Big talk from last place!" he howled at the other bench.

The Hurricanes' captain pointed at the scoreboard. "We're not in last place anymore — or can't space hicks count?"

That's when the Hurricanes' coach stepped in. He said, "That's enough! Show some class, you guys! We're beating the pants off them. Have a little pity for those poor Martians."

I guess Boom Boom didn't mind when we were insulted by the other kids. But when an *adult* called us Martians, he lost his cool.

He jumped up onto the players' bench, shook his fist at the Hurricanes' coach, and thundered, "*Your mother wears doohickeys!*"

He got kicked out of the building. But not before half the team gave him a hug of appreciation.

Trent faced the referee. "There's still four minutes to play, and now we have no coach!"

The official looked around. "Every team has to have an assistant coach. Where's yours?"

"Yoo-hoo," came a voice. "I'm here."

High heels clicked on the metal bleachers. Mrs. Bolitsky rushed down the center aisle and came to rescue her husband's team.

The referee almost swallowed his whistle. "*She's* your assistant coach?"

Alexia stood up. "You got a problem with that?"

The linesman took one look at Mrs. B. and crashed into the glass.

I thought the bleachers were going to tip over when every dad on both sides leaned left to get a look at our spectacular assistant coach.

Efficiently, she sent a line out, and play resumed. This time, the Hurricanes were just as disorganized as the Stars. Alexia caught sight of the puck handler staring at Mrs. B. instead of the play.

Wham!

It was a legal check, but there was probably some revenge mixed in there too. Alexia stole the puck and started down the right wing.

A figure in green came up alongside her, then swerved behind as she crossed the blue line. The defense moved up to challenge her.

Alexia faked a deke, then dropped a soft pass to the teammate behind her.

It was Trent, in perfect position. His stick was already pulled back.

Pow!

The slap shot whistled in on goal, rising all the way. The goalie never even saw it until it caught the top corner and fell to the ice. 12–1, Hurricanes.

We semicelebrated. At least the shutout was broken.

"Nice drop pass," Trent said shyly as the scoring line returned to the bench.

Anybody else would have answered, "Thank you." But Alexia was highly insulted.

"If I'd known it was you back there, I never would have passed!"

He was genuinely amazed. "But why? We scored!"

32

"*We* didn't score," she said quietly. "*You* scored. That was the whole idea, right? To make you look good and us look bad?"

Trent Ruben didn't have reverse volume control. When he blew his stack, he yelled his head off.

"*I* made *you* look bad? You guys are flopping around like fish out of water! Your net looks like a puck factory! Offsides and line changes may as well be rocket science to you! Your coach speaks his own language, and nobody else is in on it! And let's not forget that one of you *exploded* on a penalty shot! And *I'm* making *you* look bad? You guys are the undisputed world champions of the looking-bad hall of fame!"

Then the Stars got their first real break. The buzzer sounded to end the game.

Chapter 5 [[[[[

What a disaster!

Oh, sure, I know that a Cinderella team never starts out great. But to be as hopeless as the Stars, the real Cinderella would have to have had a hundred and fifty wicked stepsisters instead of just two. And each of them would have to have been armed with a rocket launcher.

Not that I was giving up, of course. But I came to a decision on the very night of that first game. I could ride the emotional roller coaster of the Mars Health Food Stars. But not without jawbreakers.

"Clarence, dear, why are you leaving so early?" My mother caught me creeping to the front door on Monday morning. "The school bus won't be here for half an hour yet."

"Well —" I'm a really bad liar. "I like being early. It's a beautiful day."

I opened the front door. Sleet cut into my face like ice-cold needles.

I hardly noticed the bad weather. I was a man with a mission. My destination: Toute Sweet, where they had the best selection of jawbreakers in Mars, and probably Waterloo too.

Mr. Gunhold was just opening up when I came racing through the door. I almost cheered when I saw he had a big supply of Grape-ola Mega-Bombs. These were among my all-time favorites. They were like regular jawbreakers, but with real grape juice explosions inside. I loaded up a sack faster than you could say "cavity."

At the cash register, Mr. Gunhold took my bag instead of my money. He shook his head sadly. "Sorry, Chipmunk. You can't shop here anymore."

"What? Why?"

"Your mom called last week. Bad dentist appointment, huh?"

"No fair!" I whined. "It's — like — discrimination against people with weak teeth!"

Mr. Gunhold shrugged. "You think I like losing my best customer? But your mom's the boss. That's it."

I ran out of the store. This stank, but it wasn't over

yet. I knew there was a pretty good selection at the convenience store. The clerk was someone I didn't recognize. She was just about to hand me my Licorice Cannonballs when she caught sight of the name on my book bag.

"Adelman — are you the kid they call Chipmunk?"

"Of course not!" I babbled. "I just borrowed his knapsack!"

She didn't believe me. "The boss left a note on the cash register. It says you had eleven cavities at your last checkup."

"Well, then, I've suffered enough, right?" I argued. "That was a lot of drilling, you know!"

"I could sell you some sugarless gum," she offered.

Sure. When you're looking for a jawbreaker, you don't want to hear the word *sugarless*.

I had one last chance. The gas station on Demos Avenue had a minimart. Their jawbreakers were lousy, and usually pretty stale. But this was desperation time.

I was barely inside the door before the clerk grabbed all the jawbreakers and hid them behind the counter. "Forget it, Chipmunk," he laughed. "Your mom told the whole town."

"I'll pay extra!" I pleaded.

He was unmoved. "Oh, boy, this is my chance to make a whole quarter! Hey, isn't that your bus?"

I had to chase the bus halfway to the bridge, waving and screaming in the freezing rain.

I was in a bad mood, right? Well, I was Mr. Jump-for-Joy compared with the zombies on the school bus.

"Thanks for telling Mrs. Kolodny I was back there running!" I snarled sarcastically.

"You've got ice in your stupid eyebrows!" Josh snapped back.

Whoa! Josh was the most easygoing kid in Mars. If he was this touchy, his sister, Alexia, must be a walking meltdown!

Wouldn't you know it? The only empty seat was right next to her. I slid into it, trying to be invisible.

The windows rattled as we went over the bridge. Otherwise, the bus was as quiet as a tomb.

"All right," Alexia said suddenly, "fork it over."

I stared at her. "Fork what over?"

She glared at me. "If someone's writing about what a lousy team we are, I want to know in advance what the *Gazette*'s going to say."

I had to protect freedom of the press. "A reporter's notes are private!"

She lifted me up by the collar and yanked the notepad out of my pocket. Then she dropped me back onto the seat. I almost got shish-kebabed by my own pencil.

Her face got a little darker with every page she flipped through. "This is awful!" she told me.

"What was I supposed to put?" I challenged. "That you *won*?" But I knew what she was talking about. After the game I'd interviewed some of the Waterloo kids, and those quotes were pretty rough:

"Everybody knows those Martians don't belong in our league!"

"What a bunch of space clowns!"

"They should be kicked out! They're bringing down the quality of play!"

And the unkindest of all:

"Trent Ruben or not, I guarantee they won't win one single game!"

"Those aren't my words," I pleaded. "That's what people really said!"

She returned my book. It kind of stung when it bounced off my nose.

"Be sure to keep those notes," she ordered grimly. "Every single one of those guys is going to eat his own quote when our team gets good!"

Good? The Stars would have to improve five hundred percent to get to be *bad*!

We pulled into the school yard. I knew something

was wrong because we didn't get the usual space-port docking jokes from Mrs. Kolodny. It didn't take long to find out why.

A crowd was gathered in front of our parking space. It parted just as we lined up at the bus door.

There was a pile of hockey equipment on the side-walk — jerseys, gloves, pads, sticks, even skates. At the center of it all lay a clothing-store dummy, stark naked. Across its back was written:

MARTIAN PENALTY SHOT

Cal elbowed Jared. "Get it? You took a penalty shot, and all your stuff came off!"

"It wouldn't have happened if we'd practiced," Jared muttered under his breath.

If Cal thought it was funny, the Waterloo kids considered it the most hilarious joke in the history of the world.

We slunk into school, totally humiliated.

There was a Mars bar wrapper taped to my locker. Empty. Those Waterloo jerks didn't even have the decency to include the candy. Mars bars can be almost as hard as jawbreakers if you stick them in the freezer.

On the way to English, I noticed a lot of other lockers with wrappers on them. It was amazing the lengths people would go to just to insult our town.

Anyway, I don't want to make any accusations, but when I got to English class, there sat Happer Feldman and Oliver Witt. They were both munching on candy bars. I mean, everyone's innocent until proven guilty, but those guys were *guilty*. They were lucky Alexia didn't put two and two together when she got to class. Trent sure did.

"Mars bars. Real mature, you guys." He took his seat beside his old line mates. "I heard you beat the Flyers on Saturday. Way to go."

"No thanks to you," said Happer resentfully.

My ears perked up. I have reporter's ears. It's almost like my ears have a nose for news. It's going to be a great skill for doing interviews in the locker room after Stanley Cups and Super Bowls when I'm on staff at *Sports Illustrated.* I just block out the other sounds, and focus on one conversation.

"No thanks to *me*?" Trent repeated. "No thanks to your uncle, the league president! It wasn't my idea to change teams."

"We hate being the HOG line," Oliver complained. "We want our *T* back."

"You guys both scored," Trent commented.

"We would have had hat tricks with you at center!" exclaimed Happer. "Gavin Avery is a puck hog. He thinks passing is what happens when you don't flunk!"

"The worst part is watching you trying to play with those Martians," added Oliver. "They stink."

"I know," Trent said sadly. "But they're not as bad as they look. You wouldn't believe their practice rink. It's like skating on frozen mashed potatoes! I almost killed myself!"

Happer shook his head. "It's humiliating to have them in our arena! They can't skate — they can barely stand up. And there's a *girl* on the team!"

"Trust me. I almost swallowed my helmet when I saw her," said Trent. "I didn't know girls were allowed in the league."

"They *aren't*," moaned Happer in true pain. "At least, they *weren't*. But my uncle says the league can't keep anybody out. Not without risking getting sued."

Mrs. Spiro came in, so the three lowered their voices. I had to strain to eavesdrop.

"You've got to quit," whispered Oliver.

"Quit?" Trent stared at him. "You mean not play hockey?"

"It won't be for long," Happer reasoned. "Pretty

soon they'll start putting together the all-star team. You think they want to go up against the other leagues without you? So you just say, 'Sure, I'll come back. But only to the Penguins.'"

"You wouldn't believe how much time I spent saying stuff like that to my dad," replied Trent. "You know what he told me? 'Nobody's bigger than the league. You play where they put you.' So I play for the Stars. I don't like it, but it's better than not playing at all."

"You mean you're not even going to *try*?" asked Happer in horror.

"There's nothing to try," Trent insisted.

It looked like there was going to be a pretty big argument, when Mrs. Spiro started to speak.

"All right, class. You've had the weekend to think about choosing partners for the research project. Let's hear the group pairings."

I put up my hand. "Mrs. Spiro, you remember we agreed that my article on the hockey team would count for my project."

She nodded. "Yes, Clarence. So you're working on your own. Who's next?"

She noted a few groups of two and three. And then Happer leaped to his feet.

"Mrs. Spiro, I'm doing my project with Oliver."

She smiled and wrote it down. "And, of course, Trent?"

"No. Just me and Oliver. We're teammates."

My reporter's sense was tingling like I was being eaten by fire ants. A whole new substory was being born in front of my eyes — headline: *Mutiny on the HOT Line.*

Trent hissed, "What did you say that for?"

But he already knew the answer.

Mrs. Spiro checked the list. "That's everybody except Trent and Alexia." She beamed at each of them. "I have an idea. Why don't you two join forces?"

Alexia and Trent locked eyes. It was so obvious. They would rather be stir-fried than partners.

Mrs. Spiro saw it too. "Very well. You can each work on your own."

Chapter 6 \ \ \ \ \ \

Coach Bolitsky pulled a few strings and got the Stars some practice time at the community center. He knew the most important thing was getting his players comfortable on the smooth ice surface. Once they could skate without thinking about it, they could concentrate on hockey.

So I wrote in my notebook: *Practice 2: Skating.* Then I crossed it out and put *Not Falling*, since that was what the coach really had in mind.

The problem was that the Stars were totally down. They moped through the drills in slow motion. Josh moved as if his goalie pads weighed three tons each. Alexia had her chin stuck out like she was going to punch the first person with the gall to wish her "Good morning." And as for Trent — well, he had lost his team and his friends, both in the same week. If misery was snow, Trent was Antarctica.

Boom Boom couldn't ignore the unhappy mood. He blew his whistle and faced his players. "All right, I know it's a depressing thingamajig to lose."

"We didn't just lose, Coach," Josh pointed out. "We got skunked."

"Skunked by a last-place team," added Jared.

"Listen," said the coach. "When I was playing for the Boston Whatsits, we were going all the way to the Stanley Cup. Then, three weeks before the first doohickey of the playoffs, I got traded to the worst team in hockey."

What a great coach! Boom Boom was telling a story from his own NHL career to cheer up the Stars.

"And you worked hard and turned around a struggling team?" I asked, my pencil poised for note making.

"No, we went on a twenty-six-game losing streak," he replied. "The next season, I got sent down to the minors. I had to sell my car to pay for a bus ticket." His bulging eyes turned tragic. "Come to think of it, it was the worst heejazz that ever happened to me." And he skated over to the bench and sat with his head in his hands, the picture of dejection.

He was in such a blue funk that the players started practicing again, just to get his mind off that terrible memory. And when the coach perked up a little, they skated even harder, hustling up and down the ice.

"That was smart, Coach," I congratulated Boom Boom. "Using psychology to get the team working."

He looked completely blank. "Psychology?"

Anyway, whether the coach did it on purpose or not, the Stars were having a pretty good practice. I upgraded *Not Falling* to *Skating*, and even to *Skating Not Bad*, which was a miracle after Saturday.

They went forward, backward; they did crossovers, left and right; stops, turns, and all kinds of stretches and knee bends.

This was the boring part of being a sportswriter. Drills like these were important if a team was going to improve. And no one was more thrilled than I was that the Stars seemed to be getting better. But as for watching it? Yawn.

I guess my mind was drifting a little when the hole in my cheek opened up again. Then it hit me. My mom may have warned all the stores in Mars not to sell me jawbreakers. But I was in Waterloo now — with money in my pocket and time to kill.

There was a big gourmet deli right across from the community center. The second I was in the door, I knew it was my lucky day. Jackpot! They had Lotsa-Balls, a giant bag of assorted jawbreakers. All the best ones too — Grape-ola Mega-Bombs, Lava-Balls, Choco-Spheres, Guava-berry Mouth Manglers, and even Ultra Quarks, which taste like a real peanut butter and jelly sandwich!

Okay, six dollars was kind of steep for a bag of candy. But I was cut off at home. I had to take my opportunities where I found them.

I hefted a package — wow, heavy! — and headed for the cashier. I stopped short. For there, taped to the side of the register, was my grade-five school picture from last year. They were on the lookout for me, just like in Mars!

I swerved away from the counter and staggered behind the hot-soup steam table. When had Mom joined the CIA? She must have given my photo to every candy store near the school and the arena!

Sadly, I put back my Lotsa-Balls. Feet dragging, I trailed out of the deli and across the street to the rink. The team was still working out, but Jared was in his sneakers, moping around the entranceway.

"How come you're not on the ice?" I asked.

"I got in trouble," he admitted, shamefaced. "Instead of doing crossovers like coach said, I took a penalty shot. I need practice on my penalty shots."

No kidding. "Did your clothes fall off?" I laughed.

"I didn't get that far. Coach threw me off the ice. Now what am I supposed to do for the rest of practice?"

And then it came to me: My picture was on that cash register, but not Jared's.

"Listen, you've got to do me a favor! Take this money" — I pressed the six dollars into his palm — "and go over to the deli. I want you to buy me Lotsa-Balls. Got it?"

"Why can't you get it yourself?" Jared asked.

I whipped out my notebook. "Too busy. Now remember — Lotsa-Balls."

He shuffled off.

I turned my attention to the ice just in time to see Alexia level Trent with a body check that would have derailed a train. If Trent didn't work up the guts to throw a few checks of his own, he wasn't going to make it through the season. Not in one piece, anyway. The glass was still vibrating from the hit when Jared came back from the store. He handed me a large paper bag.

I felt it, and did a double take. "Why is it hot?"

He shrugged. "How should I know? It's *your* favorite thing."

I tore away the bag to reveal a clear plastic container.

"It's *soup*!" I cried, completely bewildered. "I told you to buy Lotsa-Balls!"

"That's what I asked for," Jared insisted. "And this is what they gave me." He peered into the container. "There's lots of balls in there."

"What?" I checked the label on the lid. "But they're *matzoh balls*, not Lotsa-Balls!"

"There's two spoons," he said hopefully. "Can I have some?"

"You can have it all! But first you've got to go back to the store!" I reached into my pocket. Flat broke. "Never mind," I mumbled. "Eat your soup."

The Stars clattered off the ice and came up behind us.

"Hey!" exclaimed Cal. "Are those matzoh balls?"

"Well, they definitely aren't Lotsa-Balls," I sighed bitterly.

I guess a tough hockey practice really makes a person crave soup — that's a detail that you'll probably never read in *Sports Illustrated*. My six-dollar matzoh balls were passed from Star to Star. By the time the container got back to me, it was empty.

Chapter 7

I really could have used one of those Ultra Quarks to get me through the Stars' second game, which was against the Baker's Auto Body Bruins.

Trent gave us the scouting report in the locker room. "Watch yourselves, everybody. These Bruins are a lot bigger than we are, and they're the toughest team in the league." He turned to Alexia. "You should be especially careful."

He was the only guy in the room who didn't know that was the wrong thing to say.

She stuck out her jaw. "Why? Because I'm a girl?" Then her reverse volume control kicked in, and she added, "The last time I bodychecked *you*, it took you ten minutes to remember your own name."

Coach Bolitsky jumped in. "The Bruins are more

than just hard-checking whosises. They're good. They finished second last year."

"How did they do against the Penguins?" asked Josh.

"Oh, we beat them," Trent replied, "but it was a pretty close game."

Alexia rolled her eyes. "It all comes down to that, doesn't it? You used to be king of the ice, and isn't it terrible now that you're stuck with us lousy Martians."

Trent turned crimson. "I didn't say that. I *never* said that!"

The buzzer sounded, calling the teams to the ice.

Coach Bolitsky stood up and clapped twice. "Grab your thingies and get out there on the whatsit."

During the warm-up, you could see just how this game was going to unfold. The Bruins kept wandering over the center line, jostling their opponents and getting in the way.

Their captain was a big guy with an even bigger mouth — Willis Somebody. He was a seventh-grader at the junior high. He and Trent were enemies from last season, when Trent had beaten him out for the scoring trophy.

"Let's see how good you are without the Penguins behind you!" Willis snarled at Trent.

But a guy like Trent — two-time MVP — knew how to ignore that kind of trash talk. He just went about his business.

Willis kept right on yacking: "Blah, blah, rip your head off, blah, blah, mash you into hamburger, blah, blah . . ."

Alexia skated over and peered into the jerk's visor. "Does your mother like you? I don't think so."

He was thunderstruck. "A *girl*?!"

Trent was furious. "Why did you do that?" he hissed at Alexia. "Now they're going to be gunning for you all game!"

"Let them," she replied.

From the opening face-off, the Bruins set the style of play. I think my headline said it all: *Forget the Puck; Let's Play Hockey.*

But, as Boom Boom had warned, they were really good. On the opening rush, that rotten caveman of a Willis flattened Trent and steamrolled over Brian like he wasn't even there. Josh made the first save, but when the other Stars tried to get in to help, they were kept out of the play by some pretty big muscle. Willis hacked at rebound after rebound until he finally flipped the puck over Josh. 1–0, Bruins.

We almost got that one back when Brian, the fastest Star, picked up a loose puck and streaked down the ice like he'd been fired out of a cannon.

The rush was so spectacular that it took both teams a moment to realize that Brian had left the puck way back at the red line. So when he went to shoot, there was nothing there. The Bruins' goalie even went down to make a "save" — that's how real it looked!

"Great rush," snickered Kyle, his defense partner. "Next time bring the puck."

Cal found it so hilarious that the coach had to bench him until he could stop laughing. The spectators laughed right along with him. It was just like game one — the Stars were a big joke.

But when I thought about it like a sports reporter, this was totally different from game one. The Stars weren't flopping all over the place; they were skating, and skating well. Sure, they went down on the ice a lot, but that was because the Bruins threw such hard body checks. Mostly, they were handling the puck and making plays. All last week, they'd had only two shots on goal. Now they had four already, not including Brian's ghost rush, and we were only in the first period.

It was still 1–0 when Alexia got possession behind her own net and started up the right wing. Even from my seat behind the bench, I could see the nasty grin on Willis's face — right through his visor. He aimed himself like a torpedo and sailed across the ice straight at her.

Crunch!

It was a real dirty check, with lots of elbow.

I leaped to my feet, and I was half a second behind Boom Boom.

"Thingamabob! That's a two-minute thingamabob!"

The referee saw it, too, and the whistle blasted. Willis didn't even bother to argue. He started skating toward the penalty box, smiling all over his rotten face.

A green streak came tearing across the ice and took the guy down with a murderous hip check. It was Trent, and it would have been a perfectly legal hit, except that the whistle had already blown, and the play was dead.

The referee was furious. "That was deliberate! It's an automatic five-minute charging penalty!"

So the teams played four skaters a side for two minutes. Then the Stars had to hold off a power play for another three. They didn't. The Bruins scored two more goals before Trent was finally released from the slammer. 3–0, Baker's Auto Body.

I expected Boom Boom to yell his head off, but the coach never made a sound. That was okay, because Alexia had plenty to say.

"Where do you get off making yourself my personal bodyguard?"

Trent looked surprised. "He got you with a dirty hit."

"I know what it was!" she snapped. "Don't do that again!"

In the second period, something pretty amazing happened — even by *Sports Illustrated* standards.

A slap shot clanged against the crossbar behind Josh. It bounced off the side of his blocker, dropped outside the crease, and rolled right onto the stick of Kyle Ickes. Excitedly, Kyle started the rush. But his forward skating was so weak that it looked like super-slow motion. The Bruins didn't even bother to go after him. They just swooped around, laughing. It was pitiful.

Suddenly, Coach Bolitsky jumped up onto the bench. He cupped his hands to his mouth and bellowed, *"Turn around!"*

Creeping along at little-old-lady speed, Kyle stared at him. "What?"

Now all the players were yelling along with their coach. *"Turn around, Kyle!"*

Obediently, Kyle whirled around and skated backward. It was like watching a turtle sprout a jet engine and blast off. Long powerful strides propelled him down the ice. He brought the puck with him cradled in the crook of his stick.

Alexia fell in behind him, struggling to keep up.

"Go left!" she instructed, since he was flying blind. "That's it! . . . Straighten out! . . . Cut right fast!"

Kyle followed her directions, expertly crossing over his skates as he reversed up the ice.

The Bruins were completely bewildered. They had practiced for many game situations, but this was a first. How could you check a guy who was coming, but looked like he was going?

"Get him!" yelled the Bruins' coach.

All five skaters went after Kyle. And they did get him — in a crushing sandwich. But by that time, Alexia had the puck.

She passed off to Jared, who fed a breaking Trent. The rest was vintage Trent Ruben. He faked a wrist shot. Then, at the last minute, he pulled the puck to his backhand and slid it past the goalie into the net.

"Listen up, everybody!" rasped Coach Bolitsky in the locker room after the second period was over. "We're only down by two doojigs! We're still in this dingus!"

When a hooking call gave the Stars an early power play, it was starting to look like he might be right. But the Bruins' hard-hitting style made them the best penalty-killers in the league. Rush after rush was turned away, and the Stars were forced to waste time chasing the puck all the way back to their own end. Kyle even tried another backward attack, but he went off course and skated full-speed into the boards.

The power play was pretty much fizzling when Trent got the puck at center ice. "Don't go offside!" he howled at Cal, who was heading for the blue line like an express train.

Trent did the only thing he could to keep the play onside — he dumped the puck into the zone before Cal got there. It went into the corner at a funny angle, and when it came out, it landed right on Cal's stick.

Cal was so surprised to see it there that he didn't get much of a shot off. But the goalie wasn't prepared, either, and he gave up a big fat rebound.

Down the right wing barreled Alexia. With her left arm she held off a defenseman. With her right, she golfed at the puck.

Thwack!

It slipped between the goalie's legs. The Stars were in striking distance, trailing 3–2.

The celebration was *huge*. No offense to Trent, but this was the first time a real Marser had scored in the Waterloo Slapshot League. And I really wish I could say that it inspired the Stars to come from behind and win the game. It would have been very *Sports Illustrated*.

But real life isn't like that. Instead, the Bruins got

chewed out for being scored on by a girl. They came out and dismantled us. In no time at all, they'd hammered Josh for three more goals. It was enough to make you dizzy. One minute we were right in it; the next it was 6–2, Bruins.

It's kind of depressing when the game is out of reach, but you still have to play until the clock runs out. It was a sure win for the Bruins, and a sure loss for the Stars, and nothing was going to change that. So play got sloppy.

Then, with less than a minute to go, that rotten Willis got a breakaway down the left wing. It just bugged me that this creep was going to get a chance for a hat trick — three goals in one game.

The Stars were all caught up-ice. Josh was a sitting duck.

"No-o-o-o!!"

Alexia came out of nowhere. She flashed across the ice at a sharp angle, crouched low, and drove her shoulder up into Willis's stomach.

With a terrified scream, the speeding captain went flying. He sailed first over Alexia, and then over the boards, landing upside down in the middle of the Bruins' bench. His teammates dove for cover, scattering everywhere. Not a single one was left upright. In a bowling alley, it would have counted as a strike.

The buzzer sounded. Final score: 6–2, Bruins.

The locker room was a pretty quiet place after the high fives from Alexia's body check had died down. There was no hum of conversation.

Josh was putting way too much muscle into whacking the snow off his pads. "Six more goals," he muttered. "I've let in eighteen in only two games. That's a goals-against average of nine."

"After all our practice," mourned Kyle, "if this is the best we can do, we must really stink."

Trent looked surprised. "We played a thousand percent better than last week."

"We don't need you to pretend to be loyal to us," Alexia growled. "We may be Martians, but we can read a scoreboard."

"It's not loyalty, it's common sense," Trent said sharply. "The Bruins are great, and we stayed with them for two and a half periods. That's real improvement."

Nobody said anything, but the Stars stood a little bit taller.

Coach Bolitsky burst in. "You're all invited to Mars Health Food for seaweed burritos and whatchamacallits." He added, "You too, Trent. I'll drive you home later."

"Uh — no thanks, Coach." Trent looked uncomfortable. "I'm — busy."

Alexia was all sarcasm. "Way to show team

spirit!" The girl who had knocked down the entire Bruins team with a single check slung her white skates over her shoulder and marched out the door.

Josh's eyes met Trent's.

"Still think you need to protect her?" the goalie asked with a wry grin.

Trent shook his head. "I always thought the Bruins were the toughest team," he commented. "I was wrong. The toughest team is whoever's got your sister!"

When Trent Ruben is a pro player, and Alexia Colwin becomes the first woman to make it to the NHL, *Sports Illustrated* is going to beg me for that quote!

||||| **Chapter 8**

To the President
Lotsa-Balls Candy Corporation

Dear Mr. President,

I am writing to order your fine products by priority mail. Please send me twenty dollars worth of assorted jawbreakers, with extra Ultra Quarks if possible. Note: This is a ****RUSH**** order.
P.S. — Please be careful not to send matzoh balls.
Signed,

"Clarence," called my mother. "Get your coat on. You're going to miss the school bus."

Like I cared. This letter had to go out *today*. What name should I sign? If a parcel came marked

61

Adelman, the post office would give it to my mom. That would mean twenty dollars down the drain, and a whole lot of great jawbreakers in the garbage! I shuddered. The thought of Ultra Quarks going out with the trash gave me chills.

"Clarence —" My mother's footsteps pounded on the stairs.

Oh, no! She was right outside my door! If I got caught with this letter —

I signed the first name that came to mind: Bobby Orr, my favorite old-time hockey player. Then I stuffed everything into an envelope and sealed it quickly.

I kept the letter hidden while she hustled me out of the house. I almost left my reporter's notebook. That's the kind of rush that was on.

Then I had a choice. I could either get my order in today's mail or make the bus in time.

I ran for the mailbox. I watched the bus roar over the bridge without me. The Waterloo Transit wasn't due for another hour. And I didn't think it was a good idea to beg a lift from Mom. Not unless I wanted to hear a lecture.

So I walked the two miles to school. Wouldn't you know it? In all the excitement, I'd only brought one glove. I almost froze off my note-making hand! To-day of all days, when I was going to need to make a lot of notes! I was supposed to start my player interviews at recess. I needed my hand unfrozen and ready to fly.

The interviews were my newest idea. I had lots of scores, and stats, and game highlights. But I wanted my readers to get to know the Stars from the human side. So I asked personal questions. And I got to hear that Brian's dad has athlete's foot; when Kyle was two, he wanted to be a dog when he grew up, so he ate all his meals under the dining room table; Mike Mozak collects hotel soaps, and is branching out into shampoos and shower caps.

But I also got some pretty good quotes, like Josh's: "I *know* we're getting better. It's only a matter of time before we start winning."

Or this classic from Jared about his disastrous penalty shot: "I can't figure out what went wrong. There must have been a cross-breeze." What do you say to a line like that? It takes a pretty stiff breeze to rip someone's equipment clean off. But even more important, where does this tornado come from inside a closed arena?

And Cal kept my pencil busy: "How can I be 'offside'? Everything's on *some* side! If I'm not on one side, I'm on the other!" He also told me his all-time favorite knock-knock joke, but I guess I wrote it down wrong, because I don't understand it.

I interviewed on.

"What do you want to know that for?" Trent demanded suspiciously when I asked him his favorite color.

"You'd better get used to questions like this if you're going to be a hockey player," I advised him. "*Sports Illustrated* loves the little details."

He thought it over. "Blue, I guess. No — put green. Stars' colors."

I wrote it down, and grinned at him. "Team loyalty?"

He made a face. "When my so-called friends from the Penguins read the *Gazette,* I want them to see that I'm doing just fine."

I felt the sharp tingle of my reporter's sense. There was a story here somewhere.

"So —" I struggled for exactly the right question. "Do you consider yourself more a Star or a Penguin?"

He looked really uncomfortable. "I don't know. I mean, I'm trying to be a good Star. But getting kicked off the Penguins — that wasn't fair."

I nodded, mostly because I felt sorry for the guy. "Of course, that wasn't the Stars' fault," I couldn't help adding.

"I know that," he said drearily. "And I apologize

to you guys if I'm not as loyal as I should be. The whole thing just stinks!"

I had to agree. "I guess it didn't help much when Happer and Oliver booted you out of their group in English class."

"Don't remind me!" he groaned. "That project is driving me crazy! I'm doing research on the Selke Trophy — you know, for the best two-way player in the NHL. There are two books about it in our library. But I can only get my hands on one. So I'm stuck with half a project."

"Too bad." I yawned. I didn't think *Sports Illustrated* would really want to know about missing library books. This was even worse than Brian's stories about his pet caterpillar. The problem with these personal details was that they could be so *boring*!

But I only had one more interview to go. I had saved Alexia for last because, frankly, she scares me. She sure didn't have much patience for the press.

"Get lost, Chipmunk," she told me when I tracked her down in the cafeteria at lunch.

"Aw, come on," I wheedled. "You're the only girl in the league. The public wants to know about you."

"Okay," she sighed, "here goes. My favorite color is black; my favorite food is fried poison; and my hobby is answering stupid questions."

I actually wrote half of it down before I realized she was putting me on. I started to walk away.

"Come back, Chipmunk. I'm sorry." And I knew she meant it, because she said it quietly. She pointed to her tray. "Have a french fry. I'm in a rotten mood. I wasted the whole morning in the library, waiting for some idiot to return *Great Winners of the Selke Trophy*."

I stared at her. "You mean the NHL award for the best two-way player?"

She nodded. "It's my topic for the research project. I'm kind of impressed you've heard of it, Chipmunk. You must be a true hockey fan. Not like that showboat Trent Ruben. All he cares about is making himself look good. What would he know about being a two-way player?"

"Well, actually —" I began.

She cut me off. "I've checked out *The History of the Selke Trophy*, so I've done all the research on how the award got started, and all that stuff. But I can't finish my project without that book about the winners. And whoever's got it isn't bringing it back."

I was just about to tell her, "Trent has it," when my reporter's sense tingled.

Hold on! This could be part of my story about the Stars. If I told Alexia and Trent that they'd picked the same topic, I'd be *making* the news instead of reporting it! Good reporters observe; they don't mix in.

My mind raced, and I realized there wasn't any rule about dropping hints.

"Why don't you get Mr. Lambert to let you go on the morning announcements?" I suggested. "Then you could ask who's got the book."

"And give the Waterloo kids another chance to wisecrack on the girl from Mars who thinks she can play hockey? No thanks!"

So I went racing over to Trent, and tried the same thing out on him.

He just shrugged. "I don't want to go on the announcements. For all I know, that book was stolen five years ago."

The best I could do was walk away from the two of them, and hope that they didn't both flunk English.

At times like this, the hole in my cheek yawned like a cavern. It's a huge responsibility being a reporter.

Chapter 9

Interviewing Boom Boom Bolitsky was like talking to someone from Uzbekistan and having him answer in his native language. From what I understood, the Stars' coach was born on a whatsit farm outside Mars way back in the year whenever. He had two brothers and three whatchamacallits. His father raised whatsits, but the farm also produced doohickeys and thingeroos. His mother brought in extra money by selling gizmos.

After a while, Mrs. Bolitsky took pity on me and came in to act as translator. And if it's tough to interview Boom Boom, interviewing his wife is downright impossible. She's so stunningly awesome that you just have to stare at her. I mean, she told me *everything* — all about how they first met, and the coach's NHL career. After about twenty minutes, I looked down at my notebook. I had written exactly one word: *Trees.* To this day, I have no idea what that was supposed to mean.

The Bolitskys were just about the nicest people in the universe. I mean, I wasn't even on the team. But they treated me the same way they treated their players — like family. Man, bouncing around in the back of that health food truck, holding on for dear life to a sack of oat bran, made you feel like you really *belonged.*

The Bolitskys seemed to love spending time with us and serving us snacks and dinners. It was an unwritten Stars' rule that we would never tell these two terrific people how truly awful their food was.

So we ate. And we pushed it around to make it look smaller. The smart ones wore clothes with big pockets so we could hide the really gross stuff and throw it away at home. We were all jealous of Cal, who had one of those twenty-one-pocket safari vests. He could stash away a whole tofu potpie and still have room for six organic carrot muffins.

"Wow!" exclaimed the coach's wife. "You're really the clean-plate club." She placed a fresh tofu potpie in the center of the table.

It was Friday, and the team had just come back from a practice at the community center in Waterloo.

The coach seemed thrilled with how the workout had gone.

"Your skating is really getting stronger," he praised. "I'd stack you up against any thingamabob in the league. I want to work on arm strength next. First thing in the morning and before bed at night, everybody — thirty whatchamacallits."

"Push-ups," translated Mrs. B.

Jared tried to slip a piece of potpie to the Bolitskys' dog, Whatsisface.

Whatsisface refused it.

"We're supposed to pick a team captain," Boom Boom went on. "I have to hand in the name by the next league dingus. Any suggestions?"

Brian shrugged. "That's easy. Trent."

"Oh, *please*!" groaned Alexia. "I'm so sick of hearing about the magnificence of Trent Ruben."

"He's our best player, Lex," put in Josh. "The best player in the whole league."

Alexia snorted. "I can just hear the Waterloo kids laughing at us: 'Oh, the Martians couldn't even pick a captain from Mars!' Trent treats us like garbage, and we glorify him? Phooey!"

"Hold the phone," ordered Boom Boom. "This is a team doohickey, and we don't want any name-calling. Especially against someone who isn't here."

"Well, that's the whole point," Alexia argued, her voice dropping fast. "He's not here. He's *never* here. How can you have a captain who doesn't even go to your team doohickeys?"

There was a long silence as we digested this. Yeah, Alexia could be a class-A crab. But when she used her reverse volume control she had a nasty habit of being right.

"That's enough —" began Coach Bolitsky.

At that moment, the bell on the shop door jingled. We all looked up.

There, gasping for breath, stood Trent. He looked like he had run the two miles from town.

"Trent!" cried Josh, delighted.

We gave him the kind of welcome you'd give someone who was returning from a five-year polar expedition — backslaps, high fives, the works. Alexia was completely disgusted.

Trent looked frantically around the restaurant. "What a relief!" he wheezed. "You're all still here!"

"Calm down. Catch your breath," soothed Mrs. Bolitsky. She handed him a glass. "Drink this."

He must have been really thirsty, because he downed it in three colossal gulps. He began to choke.

"It's turnip cider," I whispered in his ear. "The taste goes away after a couple of hours."

Trent got his breathing under control and started to talk. "Happer Feldman just came over to my house. He told me that the Stars aren't a hundred percent in the league yet. It's only a trial membership."

"He's lying!" cried Josh. "How could he know something like that?"

"His uncle's the league president," Trent retorted. He turned to Boom Boom. "Coach? Do you know anything about that?"

Boom Boom shuffled uncomfortably in his chair. "I didn't want to worry you," he admitted. "But it's true. That Mr. Whosis —"

"Feldman," supplied Mrs. B. "He wouldn't give us full membership. Not even when Boom Boom offered to be coach *and* sponsor."

"You mean they're going to throw us out?" wailed Cal.

"Maybe not," was the most the coach could reassure us. "The next whatsit meeting is on November fifteenth. That's when they'll decide if we're in or out."

A babble of protest filled Mars Health Food. Even Whatsisface howled.

"Wait a minute." Alexia's quiet voice drowned the hubbub like a bucket of water on a campfire. She turned blazing eyes on Trent. "Happer Feldman hates your guts! How come you two are having this heart-to-heart talk about the fate of *our* hockey team?"

Trent looked sheepish. "He wants me back on the Penguins. His uncle told him that if the Stars get kicked out, they'll let me return to my old team."

"Well, congratulations," she said with false heartiness. "That's what you wanted right from the start, isn't it?"

Trent got so mad that you could almost see smoke coming out of his ears.

"What's your problem?!" he roared, as loud as she was quiet. "Since when do you have some magical power to read minds? You don't know what I want!"

"So what did you tell him?" I asked, doing my best to act like a reporter in this supercharged scene. "Happer, I mean."

Trent's eyes shot sparks. "I told him I wouldn't go back to his lousy Penguins if he promised to engrave my name on the Stanley Cup!"

"If they kick us out, you won't have any choice," Josh reminded him.

Coach Bolitsky stood up. "Mr. Whosis can only cancel our membership if he can show that we're not competitive."

"We're competitive," Brian put in. "I mean, sort of."

"We've got to prove it," Trent said firmly.

Alexia jumped to her feet. "We?" she said sarcastically. "*We?* So now that your precious hockey career is on the line, you're one of us?"

"Okay!" exclaimed Trent. "I admit it — I'm not thrilled to be here. But I *am* here. And we're in this together."

"But how can we prove we're good enough when the league hates us?" Jared protested.

"By winning," replied Trent. "They can't complain that we're not competitive if we've beaten somebody."

All eyes turned to the coach for confirmation.

"*Now* you sound like a dingus!" exclaimed Boom Boom.

"Team," translated his wife.

"We've got two games before the November fifteenth meeting," Trent went on. "There's the Flyers on Sunday, and the Penguins on the twelfth. We can't count on beating the Penguins. They're just too strong."

"We'll kill the Flyers!" cheered Cal. He looked around, worried. "Won't we?"

"The Flyers are a solid bunch of whosises," said

Boom Boom. And you could just hear the years of experience from an NHL player who'd spent most of his career with his back against the wall. "But we can beat them. We have to. We've got no choice."

Chapter 10 \ \ \ \ \ \

The Stars woke up on Sunday scared to death. Of course, I couldn't know that for sure. But *I* was terrified, and I was only the team reporter. So I could imagine how the players must have felt.

Who would have thought that this routine early-season matchup would determine the fate of the hopeful new team from Mars? It was only the Stars' third game — November had barely started. How could it be do-or-die already?

It would all come down to three fifteen-minute periods — the hours of practice; the stretches and exercises; the days when so many Stars were out jogging that Mars looked like a track meet. Not to mention a certain grade-six sportswriter's story about a Cinderella team. It could be gone if the Stars didn't come up with a win today.

I shook my head to clear it. It was crazy to think this way. I remembered Boom Boom's philosophy: We *will* win because we *must* win.

As I started toward Mars Health Food, I noticed a brick on top of the bank of mailboxes at the end of our street. What was that doing there? I went over to check it out. Someone had placed it as a paperweight to keep a yellow postal slip from blowing around. I was about to walk away when I noticed the name on the paper: *B. Orr.*

I pulled the slip out from under the brick and kissed it. It was a parcel notice! My shipment from the Lotsa-Balls Corporation was waiting at the post office! The note must have gone into the wrong box because our mailman had never heard of B. Orr. It could have gotten lost! But some fine, upstanding, wonderful saint of a neighbor had weighted it down with a brick for me! And now here it was — a ticket to jawbreaker heaven! I couldn't believe my good luck.

I practically floated to the Bolitskys' store. Tomorrow, right after school, I would fill up that hole in my cheek for good. Chipmunk Adelman was back in business.

I found Boom Boom with his head stuck under the hood of the truck.

"Problems?" I asked anxiously.

He emerged, a bewildered look on his face. "I started her up because she was giving me trouble yesterday. I thought maybe she needed a new thingamajig, or one of those gizmos around the hee-jazz was sticking, or maybe there was dirt in the whatchamacallit. But today she's purring like a Rolls Royce. How's that for good luck?"

Good luck was popping up all over the place that Sunday morning. Alexia and Josh's father had just found a piece of a jigsaw puzzle that had been missing since 1978. Cal's house was mysteriously receiving all the cable TV stations for free. Brian's toothache went away. And the mouse that the Ickes family had been chasing around their basement since before Kyle was born finally had died.

"I don't want to jinx us or anything," said Jared, pocketing the dollar he'd picked up off the sidewalk on the way over, "but maybe things are finally starting to go our way."

Trent was waiting for us outside the community center. "Found my lucky skate tightener," he told us with a grin.

The Flyers were sponsored by Feathered Friends Pet Shop. They were the only team in the Waterloo Slapshot League with a mascot — a mynah bird named Fly-Boy. Fly-Boy sat in a wire cage on the bench, squawking out his only sentence, which was: "Aak! Go, Flyers!"

"Listen to that stupid thing," Trent commented during the warm-up.

Alexia shrugged. "I like birds. Especially the drumsticks."

The Stars even got the good bench — the one closer to the water fountain. We'd never had that bench before! I allowed myself to believe — just a little — that the good luck that had brought my jawbreaker shipment might be spilling over into the game.

The Stars looked very solid during the warm-up. I suppose I shouldn't have been so amazed. After all, I'd been there for every minute of every practice. But wow! The passing was crisp, the skating was strong, the shots were hard and on target, and Josh seemed sharp in goal.

They were stiff, though, because they were scared. And if you think *they* were nervous, you should have seen Boom Boom. His eyes were even wilder than usual, and his ponytail was limp and sweaty, even though it was cold in the community center.

Before the opening face-off, he called the players together for an inspirational speech. It was so full of thingamajigs, doohickeys, and whatchamacallits that a team of translators from the United Nations wouldn't have figured it out. But the emotion in his voice said it all: *This is the big one.*

From the very start, the Flyers' game plan became obvious: Stop Trent and you stop the Stars. He was stick-checked, poke-checked, bodychecked, and double- and triple-teamed. But it didn't take long before Trent figured out a way to make them pay. A gang around Trent meant that Alexia and Jared were in the clear.

Barely a minute into the game, our center drew three Flyers into the corner with him. He took a pretty heavy pounding. But he managed to get the puck out to Alexia, who was all alone at the face-off circle. She raised her stick to fake a slap shot. Then, at the last second, she feathered a pass to Jared, who was steaming in on goal. He swooped forward just in time to reach out and tip the puck into the corner of the net.

The Mars fans roared to their feet, and I roared with them, fumbling for my pencil. I had the perfect headline: *Stars Draw First Blood.* We'd never had a lead before! If we could build on it, and hold it, we could save our team!

The Stars celebrated, but Jared was out of control. For him, this wiped out the catastrophe of the penalty shot way back in game one. Long after the cheers of the crowd had died down, the sound of his joy still echoed in the arena — that and the constant message from Fly-Boy, the mynah bird mascot:

"Aak! Go, Flyers!"

It wasn't too long before the Flyers struck back. They had Terry Compton, the best defenseman in the league. He was only the size of a third-grader, but, boy, could that kid skate! He made an end-to-end rush and wound up one-on-one against Kyle. While he was skating backward, Kyle matched the speedster step for step. But when Kyle turned around, it was all over. He fell flat on his face, and Terry had a clean breakaway. He made a textbook fake and stuffed the puck between Josh's legs. 1–1. Our lead was over.

"Aak! Go, Flyers!"

Despite the tie score, the Flyers looked surprised, and maybe even a little nervous. They had expected the league joke to be an easy win. And here were those same Martians, playing hard-checking, hard-skating hockey.

There were goof-ups, of course. Like the time Jared skated full-speed into the boards and almost put the butt end of his stick through his stomach. Or when Kyle got confused on one of his famous backward rushes. He made a wide U-turn and bore down on his own net. Since he was facing the wrong way, he couldn't see that the goalie he was shooting at was Josh. Alexia had to race over and bodycheck her own teammate to keep him from making a play.

Back on the bench, Kyle was outraged. "Why'd you have to hit me?"

"You were about to score," Alexia explained quietly. "For the other team."

He looked resentful. "Somebody should have warned me."

"*Everybody* was warning you!" she shot back. "We were all screaming our heads off!"

"I didn't hear anything but the Flyers' mascot," Kyle insisted. "That voice! It could shatter glass!"

It was true. That stupid bird was getting louder and louder. There must have been two hundred and fifty people in the arena, most of them yelling. And that piercing birdcall cut through every sound.

"Aak! Go, Flyers! Go, Flyers!"

The person it bothered the most was Trent. "When I was a Penguin, we put a mynah bird poster in the locker room whenever we played the Flyers. We used to throw darts at it between periods."

Alexia shot him a sweet smile. "I wonder whose picture they throw darts at now."

"Let's not let the bird get into our heads," Boom Boom warned the team. "This thingamajig is ours to win!"

Cheers greeted both teams as they came back to start the second period. This was shaping up into one of the most well-matched, exciting games anyone had seen all year. The fans from Waterloo and Mars had one thing in common: They liked good hockey.

The Flyers scored first to take a 2–1 lead. Then Brian was called on a tripping penalty. Things were tense for the Stars. If they allowed a goal on the power play, it would put them down by two. In a tight game like this one, that could be an awfully deep hole.

I set my jaw. I had to stop all this negative thinking. To clear my mind, I pictured the little wood-frame Mars post office. In there somewhere was a big box of Lotsa-Balls with my name on it. Well, actually, it was Bobby Orr's name. But the jawbreakers were all mine.

Coach Bolitsky switched Alexia to defense and sent her out to join Kyle. The puck was dropped, and the four Stars skaters moved into the "box" formation to protect Josh.

The Flyers had a strong power play, mostly because of Terry Compton. He parked himself just inside the blue line. And you could never tell what he was going to do. He could use his lightning speed to slice in on goal, but he also had a great slap shot — not a wild cannon, but a low, dangerous sizzler.

The Stars scrambled around, trying to ice the puck. But with Terry patrolling the blue line, it was almost impossible. He intercepted Alexia's clearing attempt and fired a hard slap shot at the net.

Josh made a quick stick save, but he gave up a big fat rebound.

"Oh, no!" wailed our goalie.

The puck was dribbling right to the Flyers' center. In a split-second decision, Josh dove out and swiped his stick at the puck. But the center was able to draw it back to Terry at the point.

I was on my feet, howling. I have no idea why. Nothing could stop what was happening on the ice. Terry had the puck, and there was no one in the net.

Pow!!

A booming slap shot was on the way. Suddenly, Alexia hurled herself right into the path of the blistering drive.

Crack!!

The puck blasted into her visor and deflected over the boards and out of play. Alexia hit the ice and lay there, unmoving.

⦚⦚⦚⦚⦚ **Chapter 11**

Boom Boom went over the boards like a hurdler, and slip-slid his way to the fallen Alexia.

The referee joined him. "Are you okay, son?"

There was a brief pause, then, "I'm not your son. I'm your daughter."

The man's jaw dropped. "A *girl*?!"

An electric shock couldn't have brought Alexia back to life any faster than those two words.

She sat bolt upright. "What do you mean by that? Girls can't play hockey? Girls can't block slap shots?"

Leaning over his coach's shoulder, Josh breathed a sigh of relief. "She's okay!"

The coach was angry at Alexia. "Why would you do a crazy, reckless whatchamacallit like that?"

Alexia allowed herself to be hauled to her feet. "I had a chance to clear the zone," she explained, "and I messed up. I had to make it right."

"Aak! Go, Flyers!" was Fly-Boy's opinion.

Play resumed.

There was a sigh of relief in the arena as the two minutes expired, and Brian came out of the box. The exhausted penalty killers headed for the bench and a well-deserved rest. The second line took the ice for the Stars.

Coach Bolitsky had been working hard with this unit at the practices, and it was starting to show results. Since he couldn't keep Cal from bumbling offside, he trained this trio to play a dump-and-dig style of hockey. As soon as they had the puck past the red line, the center, Mike Mozak, would shoot it into the corner. Then the wingers would go in after it.

Cal was good at this job. He was the biggest Star, and second only to Alexia at bodychecking. On that shift, the Flyer defenseman, a junior high kid, beat him to the puck. But Cal hip-checked him against the boards. The seventh-grader fought hard to freeze the play for a whistle, but that was another great thing about Cal. He never gave up. Unable to move his stick, he kicked the puck loose. It bounced and rolled over to Mike, who passed it back to Brian at the point. Meanwhile, Cal planted himself in front of the net. With Cal blocking his view, the Flyers' goalie never saw Brian's shot until it was too late to stop it.

Tie game, 2–2.

"How do you like that one, bird?" Cal cheered as he skated by the cage on the Flyers' bench.

"Aak! Go, Flyers!"

In the third period, both teams began to step up the pace. I scribbled another headline idea: *End-to-End Action*.

There were power rushes for both sides, defensive heroics, fantastic saves. The Stars were fighting for their lives; the Flyers were determined not to lose to the joke of the league. It made for some fabulous hockey.

This was what we Marsers had always dreamed of — our team skating it out, neck and neck with the Waterloo kids.

The third period ticked down. Ten minutes to play. Then five. Then two. Would the Stars be able to break the deadlock?

And then things began to go terribly wrong.

Trent hit the post with a rocket slap shot. The drive was so hard that the puck rebounded all the way out to the neutral zone. The Flyers scooped it up on a four-man rush. Alexia went to make the check, but got tangled up with the wrong player. They both went down, leaving three Flyers moving in on Kyle and Brian.

Brian missed a poke check, and a quick pass got behind Kyle. That meant a two-man breakaway. Poor Josh could only stand there, watching helplessly, while the puck went from Flyer to Flyer, and finally into the net.

3–2, Flyers. A minute and twenty-three seconds remained on the clock.

"Don't panic!" panicked Boom Boom. He was standing on the bench, howling as the players lined up for the face-off at center ice. "Just shoot the whatsit into their end so I can pull the thingamajig!"

Pull the goalie? My heart skipped a beat. That is one of the most exciting moves in hockey. A desperate team replaces its goalie with a sixth skater for a last-minute attack.

I climbed up on my seat. I was too engrossed in the game to think about how much *Sports Illustrated* would love this.

Trent was having trouble hearing the instructions from the bench. "What did you say, Coach?"

Boom Boom cranked up the volume. "Shoot it in so I can pull the thingamajig!"

"Aak!" squawked Fly-Boy, nervous from all the shouting. "Go, Flyers! Go, Flyers! Go, Flyers!"

Trent gestured helplessly at the coach. "I didn't get that! Pull the what?"

Boom Boom ran to the far end of the bench and leaned out into the penalty box to be as close as possible to his center. His mouth was only six inches from Fly-Boy's cage. And when he bellowed, his voice was like a foghorn.

"The thingamajig! I'm going to pull the thingamajig!"

Fly-Boy flapped wildly, beating his wings against the bars of his cage. Finally, he settled back on his perch, teetered unsteadily, and chirped, "Aak! Thingamajig!"

"Time-out!" bawled the Flyers' coach. He glared at Boom Boom. "What are you trying to do, Bolitsky?" He knelt down in front of his mascot like he was seeing to an injured player. "Come on, Fly-Boy. Say it, pal. Go, Flyers!"

The bird looked right through him. "Aak! Thingamajig!"

The referee skated over. "What's the problem?"

"I demand a penalty against the Stars!" roared the Flyers' coach.

"What for?"

"It took me two years to teach this bird to say, 'Go, Flyers,'" the coach complained bitterly. "And now all he says is 'thingamajig!'"

"Aak! Thingamajig!" confirmed Fly-Boy.

"See?"

The referee's lips twitched as he looked from Boom Boom to the bird, and then back to the Flyers' coach. "I haven't memorized the rule book. But I'm pretty sure there's no such penalty as two minutes for bird deprogramming. Now get your team ready. Your time-out is up."

The Flyers' center took his place in the circle opposite Trent. Face-off!

Trent stepped into his opponent and tied him up. The puck was kicked around between their four skates until Alexia bulled into the fray. She poked it loose, stickhandled over the red line, and shot it into the Flyers' end.

"*Pull the thingamajig!*" shouted Boom Boom.

"Stop *saying* that!" howled the Flyers' coach.

Josh scrambled to the Stars' bench. Cal hurled himself over the boards and joined the stampede to the corner. This was it! The net was empty!

Speedy Brian was the first to the puck. But Terry got to him before he could make a quick pass.

"Last minute of play in the game," came the PA announcement.

I barely heard it over the screams of the crowd.

Alexia flung herself into the corner to help Brian. She knocked the smaller Terry off the puck with a hip check, and passed to Jared in the slot. Jared fired a hard wrist shot.

The goalie kicked out his leg for a beautiful pad save.

Trent fought against two Flyers for the rebound. The clock ticked down.

30 . . . 29 . . . 28 . . .

"Aak! Thingamajig!" shrilled Fly-Boy.

By now the bird's shrieks were the quietest sound in the building.

Terry tried to clear the zone with a diving poke check. But Kyle kept the puck in, and flipped it back toward the net.

16 . . . 15 . . . 14 . . .

The puck hit the ice just outside the goal crease. For an agonizing moment, it sat there, fat and inviting. Then a forest of hockey sticks was banging away at it — the Stars digging, hacking, chopping for the tying goal.

7 . . . 6 . . . 5 . . .

Terry dropped to his knees to freeze the puck, but Alexia thumped him off it with a lowered shoulder. But, in the process, she stepped on his stick. She lost her balance and crashed to the ice beside him.

3 . . . 2 . . . 1 . . .

Lying flat on her back, Alexia reached around the fallen defenseman. Using the butt end of her stick as a pool cue, she clinked the puck loose to Trent, who fired it into the corner of the net.

"Oh, *yeah*!!" I launched myself up in the air like the rocket that carries the space shuttle. But even before I came down, I noticed that the green light — not the red one — had flashed on behind the glass.

The referee waved his arms. "No goal!" he exclaimed. "The time ran out! The Flyers win!"

The Flyers fans went nuts.

I admit it. I forgot all about my pledge not to get involved in my own story.

"*No-o-o-o!!*" I shrieked, leaping onto the Stars' bench. "There was still half a second left! A *quarter* of a second! A *millionth* of a second!"

Boom Boom grabbed me before I could jump over the boards. "The heejazz doesn't work when the gizmo is on," he explained, a crestfallen look in his normally wild eyes.

"What?!"

But even as I said it, I remembered the hockey rule. The red goal light is automatically blocked out when the clock expires, and the green light came on to signal the end of the game.

Heartbreaking but true: Trent's goal had come a hair too late to save the Stars.

I still couldn't accept it. "What if the goal judge sneezed right when Trent scored, so he couldn't get the light on in time? What if he waited on purpose because he doesn't like Marsers? What if —?"

But my protests fell on deaf ears. The triumphant Flyers carried their goalie to the locker room. Boom Boom and the Stars seemed more shocked than upset — like they couldn't believe what had just happencd. They played the game of a lifetime, but still came up short.

"Aak! Thingamajig!" squawked Fly-Boy.

"That's easy for you to say," I snapped back.

Talk about good luck turning sour! Next Saturday, the Penguins were going to slaughter us. And on November fifteenth, Happer's uncle would rule that the Stars weren't competitive enough to play in the Waterloo Slapshot League.

There was only one possible headline for this situation. In my heart, I couldn't deny it: *The End of the World.*

Chapter 12 ▌▌▌▌▌

The post office in Mars opened at eight A.M. I was there at 8:01.

The clerk at the pickup window disappeared with my parcel slip and returned with a carton. I loved the *wump!* sound it made when he put it down on the counter. It took a pretty big load of Lotsa-Balls to make a good wump.

"I just need to see some identification," the man told me.

"No problem." Without thinking, I whipped out my student card and slapped it down on the counter.

"Hold it." The man frowned in perplexity. "You're Clarence Adelman. This package is for Bobby Orr."

Whoops! Somewhere in that gut-crushing hockey game yesterday, I had forgotten my fake name.

"I can explain that," I said quickly. "It's my — uh — alias."

His eyes narrowed. "What does a little shaver like you need with an alias?"

Oh, how I wished I was a better liar. "What I mean is — Mr. Orr is a friend of my parents'," I stammered.

"Why can't he pick up his own package?" the clerk asked suspiciously.

"He's a really busy guy," I babbled. "He has the same name as a famous hockey player, you know."

He took my beautiful Lotsa-Balls off the counter and stuck the box on a shelf. "You're going to have to show me a letter from Mr. Orr authorizing you to pick up his parcel." He glared at me. "And it had better not be in a ten-year-old's handwriting."

I was insulted. "I'm not ten, I'm eleven —"

He cut me off. "Watch your step, son. It's a very serious matter to tamper with the mail."

He kicked me out of the post office.

I admit it. I cried. To be so close to a jackpot of jawbreakers — I could even hear them rolling around the bottom of the box! But they might as well have been on the other side of a toxic swamp infested by killer alligators. To get that package, I'd need a letter from some guy who had the name Bobby Orr. Like *that* was going to happen!

"Hey, Mrs. Kolodny! Back here! It's me — Chipmunk! Awwww —"

I finally caught up with the bus on the bridge to Waterloo. Between losing my Lotsa-Balls and my half-mile run, I must have been a mess — eyes wild like Boom Boom's, tears and sweat mingling together in my stinging eyes.

I looked so bad that Josh got up from his seat and put his arm around my shoulders. "You're a great friend, Chipmunk," he told me. "You're not even on the team, but you're just as miserable as the rest of us."

"It's not that —" I tried to explain.

But by then Jared and Cal were there too. It was like a group hug, right in the aisle of a moving bus.

"Hey," Mrs. Kolodny called back at us. "No standing in zero gravity."

Cal thought that was hilarious. "Zero gravity!" he guffawed as we took our seats. "Get it? 'Cause we're coming in from Mars."

Nothing seemed very funny to me just then, and my jawbreaker woes were only the beginning. My Cinderella story was turning into a disaster movie. I had to meet with Mrs. Spiro to beg for an extension for my project.

Mrs. Spiro flipped through my notebook. Her brow furrowed. It double-furrowed. Every time I thought she was at maximum furrow, a new line appeared on her forehead.

Finally, she said, "I thought this was going to be a report on the Mars hockey team. This is all about jawbreakers."

"I'm going to edit that stuff out," I assured her. "There's plenty of hockey in there. See?" I pointed over her shoulder. "Here. Read about Jared's penalty shot in game one."

"But it's only two little paragraphs!" she complained. "Then you go on and on for three pages about Lava-Balls, Choco-Spheres, and Ultra Quakes!"

"Ultra *Quarks*," I corrected. And this woman was supposed to be *educated*?

She stared at me. "What's an Ultra Quark?"

I got all misty-eyed just thinking about it. "Picture the best peanut butter and jelly sandwich you've ever tasted, only it's as hard as a rock, so it can last for hours —"

She cut me off. "I'm sorry, Clarence, but how can I grant you an extension when you've been wasting your time writing about candy? I just said no to Trent, and he needed more time because he's having trouble finding materials. It wouldn't be fair to him if you got an extension over *nonsense*."

There was a knock at the door. Alexia stuck her head into the classroom. "Oh, sorry, Mrs. Spiro. I'll catch up with you later."

"No, please come in, Alexia," the teacher invited. "This meeting is *over*," she added with a meaningful look at me. "How can I help you?"

"Well," Alexia began, "I was hoping I could get an extension on my research project because there's this book —"

"Hold it!" Mrs. Spiro interrupted. "Don't you think I can see what's going on here? You, Clarence, and Trent — my only three students involved with Mars hockey — all asking for an extension." She stood up. "I realize you're disappointed because things haven't been going well with the Martian — excuse me, the new team from Mars. But your education is more important than hockey. Is that clear?"

Alexia shot me a murderous look. Like her extension was in the bag until I came along and ruined it.

When I got to my locker, I found a yellow Post-It note stuck to the metal door. I pulled it off and read the message:

It was in Trent's handwriting.

I found most of the team gathered around the entrance to the boys' room after the three-thirty bell.

"I think Trent meant *inside* the bathroom," I said to Josh.

In answer, he nodded to the far end of the hall. There, framed in the stairwell door, stood Alexia. I understood the problem right away. I mean, everybody assumed that *washroom* meant the boys'. But Alexia — well, you know.

"Have they moved the bus stop in here?" she asked sarcastically.

I suppose we did seem to be waiting in line for something.

Jared was the first to crack. "Don't blame Trent!" he blurted. "He didn't do it on purpose! We'll move the meeting!"

"Why?" she asked. Like it wasn't obvious.

"It's the *boys'* room," I said carefully, "and since you're not a boy, you can't go in there —"

"I can't, eh?" She kicked the door open a crack and piped, "You've got five seconds, and then I'm coming in!" She counted off the time, and led her cowed teammates and me inside. "Well, what do you know. I'm defying the laws of science. A girl in the boys' room." She added, "This is really disgusting. How do you guys stand it?"

Josh rolled his eyes. "I suppose the girls' bathroom has marble pillars and uniformed attendants at all the stalls."

"At least it doesn't stink," she retorted.

Trent breezed in. "Here's the deal —" he began.

Not *Hello*, or *Thanks for coming*, or anything like that. Just *Here's the deal*; the guy was all business. I took out my notebook.

"It's going to take a lot of work to get ready to play the Penguins on Saturday. And we don't have a practice scheduled until Friday night. That's not good enough."

"Excuse us for being lousy." Alexia glared at him.

Trent ignored her. "We need to hold our own practice every day after school. Who's with me?"

There was an uncomfortable silence.

Jared spoke up. "No offense, Trent, but what's the use? You yourself said we had no chance against the Penguins. That's why we had to beat the Flyers, remember?"

Trent stared at him. "I said it would be *easier* to beat the Flyers. But that didn't happen, so now we have to beat the Penguins."

Not even Josh could manage to look hopeful. "That's okay, Trent," he said with a sad smile. "You don't have to pretend that it's not all over."

"All over?" Trent repeated in disbelief. "It's *never* all over in hockey. Any team can beat any other team on any given day!"

"Sure," said Brian. "In Fantasyland."

Trent was undeterred. "I can show you superstars who played with heart even when they were down ten goals against the Stanley Cup champions!" He zipped open his knapsack and pulled out a thick library hardcover. He waved it around like a battle flag. "This is about the best two-way players of all time! Do you think these guys would ever give up?"

Uh-oh. It was *Great Winners of the Selke Trophy.*

"Hey —" Alexia's sharp eyes fixed in on the title like anti-aircraft guns. "That's my book!"

Trent frowned. "It's *my* book. The Selke Trophy is my topic for the research project."

"Why, you —" Alexia reached into her own backpack and came out with *The History of the Selke Trophy.* "*I'm* doing the Selke Trophy! I've spent the last two weeks trying to track down that stupid *Winners* book!"

Trent's face flushed red. "It's my library, too, you know! I've been tearing apart the world for *The History of the Selke Trophy*!"

"It's not my fault you stole my topic!" Alexia raged.

"You stole *my* topic!" Trent retorted.

"*Qui-et!!!*"

That was me. Okay, I went a little nuts. After watching those two bicker for three long weeks, I couldn't stand to see them tear each other's heads off. Not when the truth was right in front of their noses.

"You guys think you're so different, but you're exactly the same kind of idiot!" I yelled, flapping my notebook as I waved my arms. "That's what makes you good at hockey. You're both stubborn and competitive. You think it's a coincidence that you picked exactly the same NHL trophy to study? You both chose the Selke because that's what you value the most — grit, determination, offense, defense — the complete player!"

Everybody stared at me. When you spend most of your time as the quiet reporter, freaking out is a great way to get people's attention.

"Even if all that's true," mumbled Trent, "it doesn't change the fact that I'm going to flunk English, and it's all her fault!"

"My fault?" she snorted. "*Your* fault!"

"You're so stupid!" I cried. I pointed at Trent. "You've got half a project based on the *Winners* book —" And at Alexia. "You're through with the half on the background and history. Why don't you guys do what Mrs. Spiro suggested two weeks ago — *be partners*!"

Trent looked up in surprise. "We'd be finished."

"Already!" added Alexia. "Hmmm . . ." She regarded Trent with — dare I say it? — respect. "You really like the Selke Trophy?"

"Most important award in hockey," Trent said with conviction.

"On behalf of Coach Bolitsky and the guys," Alexia announced, "I'd like to nominate you for team captain."

"I accept." Trent grinned. "And as captain, my first official act is to resign, and to make Alexia my replacement. The Stars' captain should be someone from Mars."

"Only if you're assistant captain," Alexia insisted.

"You see how easy it is?" I exclaimed. "Trent doesn't flunk, Alexia doesn't flunk. The only person who might flunk is —" My smile disappeared. I remembered that my Cinderella team was about to be banned from the league. "— me."

Trent read my mind. "We're not dead yet, Chipmunk! But we've got to practice every day. Are we up for it?"

A loud cheer rang out in the boys' room.

"How are you going to get ice time?" I protested. "You aren't in charge of scheduling the rink in the community center."

"We've got all the ice time we need," Trent insisted. "At *our* rink. In Mars. That's the Stars' home ice."

︳︳︳︳︳ Chapter 13

Coach Bolitsky was the most surprised guy in the world when he saw the Stars practicing at the Mars ice rink that day. He was driving by in the health food truck, and suddenly, there we were. He was so shocked that he swerved into the other lane — right in the path of the five o'clock bus to Waterloo.

I still can't believe there was no accident. As it was, Boom Boom stomped on the brakes, and spun completely around. The truck wound up with its front end halfway up the steps of the Mars Farmers Collective. The back doors jarred open, and out tumbled six fifty-pound bags of wheat germ. The team scrambled into street shoes, and we ran over to help him load up the truck again.

The coach was more amazed by the practice than

by his near-miss of a head-on collision with a twenty-ton bus.

"I didn't think you guys would show up for the thingamajig on Friday, never mind practicing on your own!" he cried with a big grin. "This is fantastic! Let's get back on the dingus!"

"Back on the ice?" Trent repeated. "But, Coach, don't you think you'd better get the truck off these stairs first?"

Boom Boom thought it over. "The Farmers Collective is closed on Mondays." He shrugged. "Let me get my doohickeys."

Skates. He fished them out from behind the passenger seat, and slammed the door. The side mirror broke off and hit the cement.

"Oops," I said.

It sure didn't bother the coach. "No problem. I don't need to see what's behind me." All at once, he looked startled. You could almost see a lightbulb going on over his praying-mantis head. "But *Kyle* does!"

"Coach?" Kyle asked nervously.

Boom Boom held the mirror about three inches in front of Kyle's face. "We can attach this to your whatchamacallit —"

"Mask," Trent translated excitedly. "Then you can

go on backward rushes and still see the defensemen checking you!"

We superglued the mirror onto the bars of Kyle's cage. It looked a little weird — kind of like his head was a satellite dish. But it worked! Kyle backed up and down the ice, executing reverse dekes. He even faked out Alexia, who had never missed a check in her life. He was amazing!

"What's your secret?" Brian asked, wide-eyed.

"Objects in mirror are closer than they appear," replied Kyle.

I made half a page of notes on that brilliant hockey observation. It took me three days to realize that those words were printed on every passenger mirror in the world. By then the Stars were well into a week of the hardest workouts I've ever seen.

When I look back over my notes, it reads like every single day, Boom Boom figured out a new way to bring the best out of the Stars. I guess the coach can seem like a bit of a clown sometimes because of his bug eyes and all that thingamajigging. But, boy, he sure knew his hockey:

MONDAY: Boom Boom designs new defense system — Kyle does all the backward skating, and Brian does all the forward. Together they make one perfect single defenseman.

TUESDAY: Coach times Trent's spin-o-rama. Personal best — .38 seconds.

WEDNESDAY: Josh executes first successful split (he did splits before, but always needed two guys to help him back up).

THURSDAY: Bodychecking drill goes nuclear. Cal and Alexia knock each other out of practice. Watch out, Penguins!

After the workouts, we all ate wheat germ. Wheat germ bread, wheat germ cereal, wheat germ multigrain granola bars, and a true horror Mrs. Bolitsky called the Wheat Germ Sloppy Joe. Trent stayed for every single dinner and gagged down every nauseating bite. Afterward, he went home with Alexia to work on combining their two half projects.

At the Friday practice, I only made one note — *Who ARE these guys?* I mean, the group I saw on the ice that afternoon was a completely different team from the Martians who had lost three in a row. After a week of intense drilling on the pebbly rink in Mars, the Stars hit the community center as if their feet had wings. They flashed around like lightning, shooting and checking. If they had played this way last week, they would have destroyed the Flyers. But tomorrow they would face the Powerhouse Penguins, the most dominant team in the history of the Waterloo Slapshot League.

"You know what stinks?" complained Josh. "The Penguins have been playing in this arena ever since they learned to skate. All their games are like home games."

It was after practice, and the Stars had just clattered off the ice. The Zamboni rumbled out to begin the resurfacing.

"Yeah," agreed Alexia. "I bet they wouldn't be so fantastic on *our* rink."

"A home game for Mars," mused Trent. "That would be awesome. But it could never happen in a million years. I mean, the community center would practically have to blow up before Mr. Feldman would give the okay."

At that moment, Mrs. Bolitsky bustled in the main entrance. "Yoo-hoo!" she called, waving a paper bag at us. "I brought wheat germ muffins!"

We were sort of used to how gorgeous she was. But the Zamboni driver — I thought his eyes would pop right out of their sockets. He just forgot what he was doing and gawked at Mrs. B. The Zamboni roared clear across the ice, and out the opening in the boards.

"Look out for the whatchamacallit!" bellowed Boom Boom.

We all started yelling to translate for the coach. The Zamboni was bearing down on the panel of circuit breakers that controlled the building's electrical system. What do you call something like that?

"Look out for the thingamajig!" I howled.

"You know, the doohickey!" added Trent.

"The whatsit!"

"The heejazz!"

But the driver was mesmerized by Mrs. B. Believe me, I know the feeling.

Crunch! Zap!

The Zamboni crashed into the panel in a shower of sparks. Every single light in the community center went suddenly dark. The giant fans in the ceiling stopped circulating air. The scoreboard flashed off. The Coke machine fell silent. I tried to make notes, but I couldn't even see as far as my paper in the pitch-black.

It took me a minute to realize that something else was missing — the constant hum of the cooling units that kept the ice frozen.

The rink was *melting*!

War Zone.

That was my headline idea for the emergency briefing called by the league. The Waterloo kids and their parents were really steaming.

The problem was that the community center wouldn't get its power back until Wednesday. So all games had to be postponed until then. But the next meeting — the one to decide whether or not the Stars would stay in the league — was on *Tuesday*.

"If you postpone the dingus, you have to postpone the doohickey too," insisted Boom Boom.

"He means the game," piped up Trent from the front row of the city hall auditorium.

"And the meeting," added Josh.

"I'm sorry," replied Mr. Feldman from the stage. "This is an unfortunate incident, but the meeting is already scheduled."

"That's not right!" thundered Coach Bolitsky. "How can you penalize us because some maniac drove a Zamboni into the electrical whatchamacallit?"

His answer was a babble of protest. Finally, one of the Penguins' fathers exclaimed, "It's not *our* fault either. If you want to blame somebody, blame your wife!"

"My *wife*?!" echoed the coach in disbelief.

"Yeah!" the man insisted. "She's — you know — and the driver — well —" His voice trailed off.

Poor Boom Boom looked totally mystified. It hit me — he had absolutely no idea that his wife was such a knockout. Here he was, married to the most amazingly beautiful woman on the planet, and the only person who couldn't see it was him. Go figure!

"My wife was nowhere near that Zamboni," he said, flustered. "She was only there to bring home-made muffins for my players."

Mr. Feldman tried to keep the peace. "Nobody is blaming anyone," he assured the crowd. "It's simply not possible to rearrange the entire meeting sched-ule for the Martia — for the Stars."

"You just want to kick us out before we've had one more chance to prove ourselves!" Trent accused.

An unfriendly ripple passed through the crowd. I don't think the league people loved the idea of their best player using words like "we" and "us" about Mars Health Food. I was pretty surprised myself. For a guy who came to our team kicking and scream-ing, Trent was turning into the heart and soul of the Stars from Mars.

"You're up against the Penguins!" called someone from the back. "You don't have a prayer!"

Alexia turned and gave the Waterloo crowd a dose of reverse volume control. "That's why we bother playing the games," she said softly but clearly. "To see who has a prayer against who. Otherwise we could go straight to the trophy ceremony."

Mr. Feldman shuffled behind his microphone. "It's out of my hands. I'm sorry."

"There's only one fair thingamajig," announced Coach Bolitsky.

Everyone stared at him.

"We play the game on schedule — in Mars."

Well, that was like trying to put out a fire with a bucket of gasoline. People went nuts, arguing, screaming, waving their arms. You'd think they were voting on putting a chemical dump in the school cafeteria.

"It's against the rules!"

"The rink's not good enough!"

"All the games have to be at the community center!"

One genius even had the gall to yell out, "It's too far!"

Some of these Waterloo jerks would sooner get on a plane to Japan than cross that little bridge over the canal.

Of all people, it turned out to be Coach Monahan of the Penguins who bailed us out.

"*Quiet!*" he bawled.

Silence fell.

He looked around the packed room. "My team has no problem playing the game tomorrow at the ice rink in Mars."

"But, Coach —" cried Happer in horror.

"But nothing!" Monahan cut him off. He turned to Boom Boom and smiled with too many teeth. "We'll be there."

Coach Monahan was so *smug*! You could just tell that he figured his Penguins would destroy the Stars on *any* rink — blindfolded, with one hand tied behind their backs, and skating through a three-foot-high layer of coleslaw.

I wanted to scream, *You'll see! We'll wipe up the ice with you guys!*

But deep down I knew he was probably right.

| | | | | | *Chapter 14*

Saturday morning found us bouncing around the back of the Mars Health Food truck. To keep away the pregame jitters, Coach Bolitsky had decided to show us his childhood home.

We jounced along the rural road for about ten minutes, then turned off and stopped. Boom Boom opened the back doors, and we piled out. We were in the middle of flat, picturesque countryside, dotted with farmhouses, silos, and barns. The bright sunshine gleaming off the snow made us all squint.

I've got to hand it to the coach. The nervous tension lifted like the roof opening on a convertible.

"This is cool, Coach!" exclaimed Jared. "Which house did you grow up in?"

Boom Boom pointed to a small, neat farm cottage. "That one. See the thingamajig out front?" Between the barn and the road was a large pond, frozen to a glassy silver. "That's where I first played hockey."

"Wow," breathed Josh. "Just like the old-time legends, way back before hockey got big and glitzy."

"It sounds great," Trent mused wistfully. "No leagues, no trophies — just a bunch of kids who love the sport, skating around, fighting for the puck —"

"Oh, we didn't play with a real puck," said Boom Boom. "No one had much money back then. We used a hunk of frozen horse manure."

Cal cracked up laughing. "Horse manure hockey!" he guffawed. "Yeah! That's a funny joke!"

Alexia elbowed him in the ribs. "It's not a joke, bonehead. A lot of old-timers used to play that way."

Cal was thunderstruck. "With *horse manure*? I mean — like, well, didn't it — you know — stink?"

The coach shook his head. "Too cold. Those thingamajigs were frozen solid like granite. And we didn't wear helmets, so you had to be careful some slap shot didn't take your head off."

That was too much for Cal. He got a case of the giggles so severe that we had to pack up the truck and head back to Mars. Boom Boom decided the players needed some time alone together, so I rode up front in the passenger seat.

My head was spinning with nervous thoughts about the game. Did we stand a chance against the defending champions? I was so wrapped up in it that I almost missed the small country store coming up on the left.

The hole in my cheek sent a signal to my brain: Mom may have warned every candy shop and 7-Eleven in Mars, and even some in Waterloo, about my jawbreaker problem. But *no way* would she think of a tiny roadside joint in the middle of nowhere.

"Hit the brakes!!" I shouted right in the coach's ear.

Shocked, he squealed the truck onto the soft shoulder. I could hear the players rolling around the back as we lurched to a halt.

"What is it?" Boom Boom asked anxiously.

My mind raced. Mars Health Food sold a little gum and candy in a rack by the cash register. That meant Mom might have tipped off the Bolitskys too. I needed a lie. What would make sense to a guy like the coach?

"I — I — I've got to do whatchamacallit!"

It worked. I flew out of the truck and hit the road running. I sprinted up to the cashier. "Excuse me," I panted. "Do you sell jawbreakers?"

The man shook his head. "Sorry. Not much call for candy out here. The closest thing I've got —" He began rummaging through an old wooden crate. "I'm pretty sure I saw it yesterday — ah, here it is."

I stared at the package in the man's hands — I

mean, Looney Toons kind of staring, where your eyes bug way out of their sockets. My heart began to beat out S.O.S. in Morse code. It was an entire bag of nothing but Ultra Quarks! *Ultra Quarks!* Forty of the greatest, pinkest, most delicious jawbreakers ever made! Oh, sure, I'd heard that the Lotsa-Balls company sold Ultra Quarks by the bagful. But I'd always thought that was a myth, like unicorns or the Abominable Snowman. Yet here it was, right in front of my face!

I threw money at the cashier so fast that he thought he was being attacked. He jumped back, and dropped the bag. I snatched it up and was gone.

"Hey, kid! What about your change?" he called after me.

But I was already back in the truck, my treasure hidden under my coat. "Go! Go! Go!"

Talk about justice! After three miserable weeks without jawbreakers; of being thwarted at every turn; of disappointments just when it seemed like I was getting close — finally I had my reward. Good things come to those who wait, I guess. And just in time for the opening face-off!

Believe it or not, there was a traffic jam when we got back to Mars. All the hoopla over where to play had attracted a huge crowd of Waterloo people to town. And when we finally inched our way to the rink, there was no place to park. Seriously! Our little Mars looked like the city that was hosting the rubber match of the Stanley Cup finals. Horns honked. Drivers shouted. We had to drop the truck at Mars Health Food and walk the four blocks to the game.

I ran ahead of the team to stake out a good seat. Actually, there were no seats at the Mars rink except for the team benches. So I was looking for someplace to stand. Already people were lined up four deep around the boards. They were watching the Zamboni from the Waterloo community center doing its best to take some of the bumps and ditches out of the rough ice surface. The front end of the big machine was dented and crumpled from the collision with the electrical panel. This time the league officials were taking no chances. The Zamboni driver was none other than Mr. Feldman himself.

It was time to pop an Ultra Quark into my mouth — joy! — and worm my way through the crowd to a good spot along the boards. I tore open a corner of the bag. A brass band began to play! Okay, it was only some girl's portable radio. But it was a really big moment.

"Clarence!"

Oh, no! It was Mom, waving and beckoning. I'd blabbed so much about this game that she decided to do me a "favor" and come! If she caught me with these Ultra Quarks, I was dead meat!

I panicked. I stuffed the bag under my jacket and ran, ducking in and out of the spectators.

"Clarence, come back! It's me!" Mom was hot on my heels.

I spotted Josh by the bench, and changed course like a cruise missile. "I need a favor," I wheezed. "You've got to hide something for me —"

"Hang on a sec," he interrupted. "I just want to put on an extra shirt." He took off his jersey, his shoulder pads, and his chest protector. Then he pulled on a black turtleneck. All at once, he was struggling. "Hey, Chipmunk," came his muffled voice through the fabric. "Give me a hand. My head is stuck."

"Yeah, sure —" I began.

But at that moment, Mom rounded the corner. I had about three seconds to hide those Ultra Quarks. But where?

IIIII Chapter 15

Leaving Josh lost in the turtleneck, I picked up his chest protector. I yanked open the zipper, pulled out the foam padding inside, and dumped in my bag of Ultra Quarks.

By the time I looked up again, Mom was upon me. She helped Josh get his head through the tight neck, and glared at me. "Clarence, what's with you today? I'm calling your name, your friend is floundering around in a sweater, and you're playing with goalie pads."

"Hi, Mom." I grinned weakly.

"Thanks, Mrs. Adelman." Josh pulled on his chest protector. The jawbreakers inside made a clicking sound.

I covered it up with a severe coughing spell. "Man, this cold weather!" I babbled, helping Josh into his shoulder pads. "I'm getting sick already! Bummer!" I hauled his jersey on over his equipment and handed him his helmet and mask.

He frowned. "My chest protector feels funny."

"Here, I'll check it for you," my mother offered.

"No time!" I said quickly. "Look, the warm-up's started." I hustled him onto the ice.

My sigh of relief must have been so obvious that Mom gave me a strange look. "I'm going over to stand with Mr. and Mrs. Colwin," she told me. "I'll see you after the game."

Luckily, Boom Boom offered to let me watch from the Stars' bench, because the rink was jam-packed. I don't know how anybody was going to see much. People were craning for a better view through a crush of bodies eight or nine deep. By the time I got out my notebook and pencil, the teams were lining up for the opening face-off.

"How's it going, traitor?" called Happer from the left wing.

"Welcome to Mars." Trent grinned with a confidence I knew he didn't feel. He was scared, but he'd die before letting Happer see it.

I was hoping the Penguins would have a lot of trouble skating on the bumpy ice. And, yeah, they were a little slower than usual. But they sure weren't falling all over the place like the Stars during their first game at the community center. Instead, Happer stole the puck and fed it to Oliver. And once those guys started on a two-man rush, it was tough to stop them. They ignored their center, Gavin Avery, like he wasn't even there. Actually, they didn't seem to need him. They roared in on goal, trading picture-perfect passes. Oliver took a booming slap shot.

Josh blocked it with his body.

The Stars and their fans cheered, but I blurted out, "My Ultra Quarks!"

Boom Boom stared at me. "Your *what*?"

I'll bet my face was bright red. "Nothing." I cupped my hands to my mouth and bellowed, "Come on, Josh! Use your glove!" I mean, if he stopped every shot with his chest protector, my precious jawbreakers would be nothing but dust by the third period.

I shouldn't have worried. On the very next play, Josh missed the puck altogether. Happer squeezed a hard wrist shot right between his legs. Less than thirty seconds had gone by, and already the Penguins had taken the lead. The Waterloo fans roared their approval.

Egged on, Happer turned even more arrogant and obnoxious than before. He called Trent "traitor" every time they came within ten feet of each other. And when Oliver scored to widen the lead to 2–zip, Happer decided the blowout had begun.

"Nice shot, huh, traitor?" he sneered in Trent's face. "You wrecked our rink, but it's not going to save you. We can crush you Martians on *any* ice! What do you say to that, traitor?"

"Will you shut up?" groaned Alexia. As the right winger, she was positioned opposite Happer. "You're not just mean; you're nuts! Trent Ruben is the most loyal teammate there could ever be!"

Trent stared at her. "Me?"

Happer was unimpressed. "What do *you* know about it?" he snarled at Alexia. "Girls shouldn't play hockey! You could get hurt!"

She didn't answer, which was a dead giveaway. The next time Happer touched the puck, she tied him up and drove him into the boards so ferociously that he crumpled to the ice. It was classic Alexia — tough but clean.

Trent skated up to where his ex-linemate lay dazed and panting. "Hmmmm," he said in mock concern. "Maybe boys shouldn't play hockey. You could get hurt."

"*You* seem tough enough." Alexia grinned at him. She looked down at Happer. "But this wimp? Kind of delicate."

Happer got to his feet. "You're going to regret this," he managed in a raspy voice.

Sure enough, on the very next play, he went after Alexia. But she danced around him like a matador, and he went careening into the boards again. He did knock the puck loose, but it found its way onto Kyle's stick. Our defenseman got himself turned around, and rushed up ice backward.

Oliver tried a poke check, but Kyle caught sight of him in the rearview mirror. So Kyle backhanded the puck lightly between his legs and past Oliver. Then he wheeled around him and picked it up.

We all leaped to our feet cheering. It would have been a move worthy of *Sports Illustrated*, except that now Kyle was skating *forward*.

"Go!" I howled.

But he was already falling before the word was out of my mouth. He landed flat on his face. Luckily, the puck went straight to Trent.

I wish I had a closer look at those Penguins as they watched Trent bearing down on them full-steam. I mean, this was something they never faced last year. One at a time, Trent faked his ex-teammates out of their jockstraps, and fired a hard, low wrist shot into the corner of the net.

"*Ye-e-eah!!*" I shrieked, but you could barely hear me over the home fans. And if you think *we* were psyched, you should have seen Trent. He was racing around the ice, pumping his fist in triumph. Man, that goal must have felt good after all he'd been through!

The score was still 2–1 for the Penguins at the end of the first period. Since there were no locker rooms at the Mars rink, the two teams agreed to take turns in the warm-up shack. But the Penguins were so used to their cushy community center that nobody knew how to operate a potbellied stove. They accidentally closed the flue, and the shack filled up with smoke. They came out fanning the air and coughing.

So both teams had to shiver through intermission on the bench. I don't think the Mars fans stopped cheering for one second of the ten-minute break.

"I'm a little worried about Josh's equipment," I overheard Alexia telling the coach. "Every time he makes a save, there's this weird clicking sound."

There weren't a lot of benefits to having a coach who didn't speak English, but this was one of them. "Don't worry," he assured her. "It's probably just the heejazz in his whatsit. Come on, the second thingie is starting."

Before the face-off, Coach Monahan gave his team a pep talk that was more like a scolding. "Look at that scoreboard," he said in disgust. "This game should be *over* already. You've let the Stars hang around long enough. Get out there and blow them away."

I thought it was a pretty mean speech, but I've got to hand it to Coach Monahan. That's exactly what happened. The Penguins hit the ice *flying*. They were all over the Stars, scoring three times to open up a 5–1 lead. I know that sounds like Josh was a lousy goalie, but remember, these were the *Penguins* — the champions. They blasted over twenty shots at him. It was a miracle they only got three goals.

In the beginning of the third period, the Mars fans were deathly quiet, and the Waterloo people were pretty subdued too. I looked around at Mr. Feldman and the other league officials. They wore self-satisfied smirks. Kind of like: *Yes, this is all according to plan. Those Martians will be out of the league by Tuesday.* It made me so mad that I almost missed Alexia's comment:

"We're going to win," she said softly.

"What?" I cried. But the other players all nodded. Didn't they remember the score?

"I agree," announced Trent. "Check out the Penguins' bench. They're exhausted."

"It knocks you out, scoring all those goals," I put in sarcastically.

"They wasted most of their energy in the second

period," Trent insisted. "They're trying to skate at their usual speed on lousy ice. Plus they're freezing. They're used to playing in a warm building."

Coach Bolitsky took over the meeting. "Okay, here's the whatchamacallit." *Plan.* "Whenever we get possession, we rush. Make them keep up with us. Pass to Trent, Brian, and Kyle. They're the fastest. Got it?"

"But we're *four goals down!*" I protested.

I admit it, I folded like an envelope. I was already making notes about how the letdown of being kicked out of the league was creating team delusions. It wasn't as good as a Cinderella story, but at least it was something.

Then I heard the cheering. The Penguins were scrambling around like chickens with their heads cut off trying to keep up with Brian. Kyle's backward rushes were freaking out the defense. And Trent — well, Trent had been dominating this league since grade four, but I can honestly say I've never seen him better.

He was the first to score, on a beautiful feed from Brian. Then Trent was able to draw three Penguins off to the left wing. He found Alexia with a perfect pass that she one-timed past the goalie. Now it was 5–3.

Coach Monahan called a time-out to get his team

calmed down. It didn't help. Struggling to keep up on the bumpy ice, the tired Penguins started hooking and tripping. Again and again, the Stars went on the power play. The Penguins' net turned into a shooting gallery, until finally Cal was able to whack a rebound past the goalie.

I couldn't believe it. It was 5–4! The Stars were a single goal away from tying the game. What a comeback! But there were only two minutes left to play.

Boom Boom made a gutsy move and pulled the goalie early. This put Cal on the attack along with Trent, Alexia, Jared, Brian, and Kyle.

"No chance you tie it up," panted Happer in the face-off circle. "You're not going to have the time."

The roar of the crowd was deafening, and it was coming from Waterloo and Mars fans alike. The players were yelling, too, and so was I. And as for Boom Boom . . .

"Get the whosis! Watch out for the whatsit! Sho-o-o-ot!"

Once again, the clock was our enemy. It ticked down: A minute, then thirty seconds, then fifteen. With ten seconds to play, Oliver managed to backhand the puck out to the neutral zone. The Penguins charged after it, but Brian got there first. He stickhandled once and then made either the best or the worst pass I've ever seen. *Worst* because every single

Penguin could just reach down a stick and intercept it. *Best* because they were so caught off guard that none of them did.

The puck slid dangerously between the legs of all five Penguins and landed on Jared's stick right at the blue line.

"*Go-o-o!!*" I shrieked into the mayhem.

It was a clean breakaway.

Chapter 16

Only the Penguins' goalie stood between our winger and a chance to send the game into overtime.

Jared roared in on net.

"No-o!" cried Happer.

In desperation, he threw his stick at the charging Star. It slid between Jared's skates and knocked the puck away. The Stars and their fans howled for a penalty. Up went the referee's arm. But when the whistle blew, only one second remained on the clock.

Boom Boom was crouched on the boards like a panther about to spring. "He threw his dingus!" he bawled. "That's an automatic —" All at once, he pulled up short. "Never mind."

"No, you're right!" the official exclaimed. "That's a penalty shot!" The man took one look at Jared, and a snort of laughter escaped him. "Hey, it's you!" He chuckled. "Guess what, kid? You've got yourself another penalty shot!"

His merriment was contagious. Who could forget Jared's performance in game one? Word spread through the crowd like a brushfire.

"It's him! The same kid!"

"The one whose stuff fell off!"

"Maybe he'll end up *naked* this time!"

Pretty soon all the spectators — even the Marsers — were rollicking with guffaws.

I was horrified. "Don't they realize that the whole future of the Stars is at stake here?"

The coach tried to be practical. "Listen, Jared. Don't worry if your doohickeys fall off —"

Jared was vibrating with excitement. "Take it easy, Coach. I've been practicing."

"Where?" asked Josh.

"My driveway," Jared replied. "On Rollerblades, using a tennis ball, with my cat as the goalie."

I wasn't making a lot of notes at this point, but I had to get *that* down. If *Sports Illustrated* wants something truly original, they should print a few quotes from Jared Enoch.

Once again, the puck was placed at center ice. Suddenly, the rink turned into a very quiet place. I tried to write something about the eerie mood, but my hand was shaking so badly that I scribbled up the whole page. That's how intense it was!

Jared picked up the puck. The crunch of his skates digging into the pebbly ice was the loudest sound in Mars. I think the whole team was expecting something to go wrong, so when he came in on goal in one piece, we all started screaming. As soon as he shot, I could see it was too high. The puck went up at a sharp angle over the goalie's glove, where it hit the crossbar with a clang. But instead of bouncing up and away, it dropped straight down to land flat on the ice — I goggled — a quarter of an inch over the goal line. Tie score, 5–5.

The Stars and the Penguins were going to overtime!

The lecture from Jared was loud and long.

"You said penalty shots weren't important," he told the coach. "But I always knew they were."

"Yes, Jared," Boom Boom said patiently.

The Penguins were warming up, stretching, and getting nice and loose for sudden-death overtime.

"You wouldn't let me practice penalty shots," Jared went on. "It's a good thing I didn't listen to you. It's a good thing I have Rollerblades and a cat. . . ."

Boom Boom and his players just sat there, taking

it. They wouldn't have complained if Jared had been beating them with his stick. Thanks to that penalty shot, they were heading into overtime with momentum on their side.

But when the extra period began, the Powerhouse Penguins were playing like champions again. From the opening face-off, they forced the action into the Stars' end. Josh had to make some sharp saves to keep his team alive. Still the Stars couldn't manage to clear the zone.

Oliver took a booming slap shot that was headed straight for the top corner. Out of nowhere came Kyle Ickes. He hurled himself heroically in front of the net. The blistering drive smacked right into the rearview mirror on his mask, knocking it free. Josh gambled, swan-diving way out of position to freeze the play. When there was no whistle, he opened his glove. He had smothered the *mirror*, and not the puck! That had gone behind the net. Kyle scrambled after it.

He came out on one of his backward rushes. But when he looked to his mirror, it wasn't there.

Crunch! Two Penguins smashed him hard into the boards. Oliver golfed at the loose puck, sending a high chopper at the goal. Josh jumped up to catch it, but Happer charged right into him. The puck landed right behind Josh — two feet in front of the open net! Josh fell flat on his back on top of it.

There it was — a guaranteed game-winning over-time goal, and the only thing in the way was poor Josh Colwin. Five Penguins descended on him like tiger sharks in a feeding frenzy, checking, battling, and digging. A split second later, the Stars were all over *them*. Alexia slammed into Happer, who landed heavily on top of Josh. It was a writhing mass of bodies, sticks, gloves, little pink balls —

Little pink balls?!

"My Ultra Quarks!!" I howled. All that action must have ripped open the zipper in Josh's chest protector.

Jared was the first to trip on the rolling jawbreak-ers. He knocked over Oliver, who upended Alexia. It was like a 1920s slapstick comedy movie. Except those old films were silent. Imagine hundreds of fans screaming while the players rolled and tumbled over my Ultra Quarks. Even the referees fell.

Then I saw it: something so important that it made me forget about forty lost jawbreakers. I shouted, "The puck!"

It was right beside Josh's left pad, a big black dot amidst the smaller pink ones.

"Where?!" Every single player tried to struggle up, slipping and stumbling on the Ultra Quarks.

Trent got there first. He corralled the puck and started down the ice. All five Penguins got up and chased him. Picture it: an end-to-end breakaway with your entire ex-team in hot pursuit. But this was Trent Ruben at crunch time. No way was he going to let himself get checked from behind. He roared in on the Penguins' goalie like he was powered by jet fuel.

Now, this netminder knew Trent. He was probably expecting a "Ruben special" — a deke to the backhand. And, yeah, Trent did that. But in a lightning move I'll never forget, he pulled the puck all the way back to his forehand and slid it around the goalie and into the net.

Final score: 6–5. The Mars Health Food Stars weren't just competitive; they had beaten the undefeated defending champions of the league!

Pandemonium broke loose. I can't remember everything that happened because some of my notes got shredded in the celebration. But it was like New Year's Eve, Mardi Gras, and the Stanley Cup parade all rolled into one. The Mars fans stormed over the boards. Boom Boom hurled himself so far out onto the ice that he could have set a long-jump record. When he came down, his feet slid out from under him, and he fell right on his head, knocking himself unconscious. The players didn't even notice. They were leaping, dancing, screaming.

With the surging crowd surged my mother, right onto the ice. People were tripping all over the place, and so did Mom. There was an Ultra Quark right where she landed, not a foot in front of her. She picked it up and examined it. She sniffed it and tested it with her teeth. I could almost see her mind working like the FBI computer: Unidentified object — jawbreaker.

You can figure out the rest.

"Cla-*rence*!!!"

Busted.

Chapter 17 ⎰⎰⎰⎰⎰

STARS FROM MARS OUT OF THIS WORLD IN STELLAR 6–5 COMEBACK

by Clarence "Chipmunk" Adelman,
Gazette Sports Reporter

In the most exciting, fantastic, stupendous, not to mention totally great game in the history of hockey, the Mars Health Food Stars saved themselves from elimination by handing the Penguins their first loss in two seasons. Trent Ruben completed his hat trick at 3:21 of overtime. It was an unusual play since the ice was covered in Ultra Quarks belonging to an unknown person. . . .

Trent looked up from my copy of the *Gazette*. "An unknown person?" he queried. "The whole world knows they were yours."

"Not my mom," I replied. "I told her they fell mysteriously out of the Zamboni."

He stared at me. "The Zamboni?"

I shrugged. "It was better than my backup lie. Hailstones. Anyway, she must have believed me because we cut a deal. I'm going to brush and floss like Tommy Tooth for six months. If I get a halfway decent dental checkup, she'll let me have two jawbreakers a week."

We were on the city bus heading for Mars. We had just come from the meeting where Mr. Feldman announced that the Stars were now permanent members of the Waterloo Slapshot League.

Trent pointed to my Chipmunk cheek. "So what are you chewing now?"

I opened my mouth and pulled out a wad of gum. "Sugarless. It tastes like rubber bands."

We were on our way to tell Boom Boom the great news. The coach had a concussion after smashing his head on the ice during the celebration last Saturday. It wasn't serious, but an old friend was visiting from Boston, so he decided to skip the meeting. It wasn't like there was much suspense about it, after all. I mean, if the Stars weren't competitive, then neither were the Penguins, since we beat them. Then they'd have to kick out everyone the Penguins beat. It would make for a very small league.

Trent handed the newspaper back to me. "What did Mrs. Spiro think?"

I shrugged. "She gave me a C-plus. She said there was still too much about jawbreakers. Who cares? It's not over yet."

Trent frowned. "Sure it is."

"The *project* may be finished," I explained. "But the season's just getting started. Man, the Stars are the greatest Cinderella team in the history of hockey! And I'm going to be with you all the way, telling your story to the world!"

Trent laughed. "To our school, anyway."

"For now," I agreed. "Just wait and see. If you guys weren't twelve, *Sports Illustrated* would be *begging* me for what Mrs. Spiro calls C-plus stuff!"

"Alexia and I got an *A* on our Selke Trophy thing," Trent told me. "We're pretty good teammates — both on and off the ice." He cleared his throat carefully. "What do you think?"

I glared at him. "I've got pages and pages of notes about you guys fighting. If you're going to turn into best friends, you're going to cost me a lot of rewriting!"

Once we got off the bus, it was a footrace to Mars Health Food. I ran my fastest, but I was no match for Trent.

He burst in ahead of me. "It's official!" he exclaimed. "We're in the league for good!"

A huge cheer went up in the store.

"You should have seen Mr. Feldman when he made the announcement!" I added, panting from the run. "His face was the color of Mrs. B.'s zucchini goulash!"

The whole team was gathered around Boom Boom, who wore a white bandage around his bald crown. He ducked down in his chair to avoid the flying high fives of his ecstatic players.

Josh and Alexia were hugging and slapping each other on the back. Jared climbed up on big Cal's shoulder, flashing V-for-Victory signs. It wasn't until Brian tripped Cal, and he and Jared tumbled to the floor, that I got a good look at the coach's friend in the chair beside him. I gawked. I *goggled.*

It was Bobby Orr. I mean, the *real* Bobby Orr, the legendary Hockey Hall-of-Famer! The only defenseman ever to win the scoring title! The greatest player in the history of that position! One of the best of all time!

My mind raced. How did the coach know the incredible Bobby Orr? The answer was simple. Boston was one of the many teams Boom Boom had played for way back in the seventies! Of course he knew Bobby Orr! They used to be teammates.

Trent rushed up to the great star and asked for an autograph.

I have to say Bobby was really cool about it. "Sure, Trent. I've heard a lot about you. Congratulations on your hat trick on Saturday."

Trent practically glowed while Bobby signed a paper for him. When the Hall-of-Famer saw me rip a clean sheet out of my notebook, he reached for it.

"How about you, son? Want me to sign that?"

"Not exactly." I spit that disgusting tasteless sugarless gum into the page, crumpled it up, and tossed it in the garbage.

I turned back to Bobby, who looked a little shocked. This was probably the first time anybody had ever spit something out into a paper he was about to autograph.

"This may seem weird," I began, "but it just so happens that there's a package for you at the post office."

The legend was thunderstruck. "For *me*?"

"It's — kind of a long story," I stammered. "I can explain it on the way."

And he actually reached for his coat.

So there I was, Chipmunk Adelman, walking to

the post office with the great Bobby Orr to pick up my Lotsa-Balls.

In a world where the Stars from Mars can beat the mighty Powerhouse Penguins, I guess anything is possible.

Look for Slapshots #2

The Dream Team

For some reason, the Waterloo kids thought there was nothing more hilarious than making fun of us Marsers. They called us Martians, and space hicks, and nebula nerds. They even named the school bus *Pathfinder* after the NASA Mars mission.

The Waterloo adults weren't much better than the kids. They were more polite, maybe, but the jokes were the same.

"We are now entering Earth's atmosphere," announced Mrs. Kolodny, our school bus driver. "Prepare for docking at spaceport Waterloo."

You see? Mrs. Kolodny said that every single day! We were all so sick of it! All except Cal, who thought it was brilliant.

"Earth's atmosphere!" he chortled. "That's a riot!"

"It's been a riot every day since kindergarten," snarled Alexia in reverse volume control. "It's not a riot anymore."

There was a big crowd of Waterloo kids hanging around the entrance. They were laughing and joking and having a great time, which usually meant some poor Marser was going to get roasted.

There was a paper taped to the door. I peered over to read it:

THE GREAT MARTIAN PUCK SEARCH

Slowly, we moved inside. There in the foyer was the department store dummy they'd used to humiliate us before. It carried a hockey stick, and wore a helmet and a green T-shirt doctored up to look like a Stars jersey — number ten, Jared's number. From the stick dangled another sign:

HELP THIS MARTIAN FIND HIS MISSING PUCK. HINT — IT'S REALLY CLOSE TO HIS BRAIN.

Did I mention that the dummy wasn't wearing any pants? How can I explain where they put the "missing" puck? Let's just say that the dummy would have had a hard time sitting down.

Cal barked a laugh right in Jared's face. "Hey, Jared, did you ever think of looking *there*?"

Jared was fire-engine red. "I never found it!" he complained.

"Have you checked your hockey pants?" Josh suggested. "Maybe it slipped into one of those pockets where the protectors fit."

Jared glared at him. "My mom already washed my hockey pants! She washed all my equipment! There wasn't any puck!"

"Then it must have fallen into a pile of laundry in your basement," Brian insisted reasonably.

Jared blew his stack. "It's not in any pile of laundry! It just disappeared! It was a supernatural event of the unexplained!"

Leave it to Jared to add fuel to the fire when the joke was on him. Those Waterloo comedians howled.

The big thing at school that day was The Announcement. It was posted on the large bulletin board outside the office — the names of the players who had been chosen for the Waterloo Slapshot League All-Star team.

This wasn't just a great honor. It also meant you got to go to the tournament in Windsor to play against the select squads from fifteen other leagues.

A lot of people were gathered around the notice. Excited chatter filled the hallway, and high fives were flying in all directions. I'm kind of short, so I tried to rubberneck past the taller heads and shoulders in front of me.

"Make way for the press!" I called. It got me an elbow in the stomach and a lot of laughs. That's why I want to work for *Sports Illustrated*. No one takes the *Gazette* too seriously.

Alexia rolled her eyes. She stepped forward and plowed into the crowd like a harvester going through a wheat field. Trent and Josh waded through after her, and I slipped in between the two of them. When I looked up, there was the bulletin board.

The All-Star list was more or less what I expected. Half the kids were from the first-place Penguins, sponsored by Powerhouse Gas and Electric. I started to copy the roster into my reporter's notebook. King Diaper was on it too, and a lot of other seventh-graders. I didn't recognize all the junior high names. Trent was there, of course, and — my pencil point shattered. That was it for the Stars.

My reporter's sense tingled hard enough to electrocute me. This was a huge story. What an insult! I mean, we all liked Trent. But he was from Waterloo. This meant that not one single Marser had made the All-Star team. Okay, Josh had a lousy goals-against average. And I suppose Jared was better known as a joke than a winger. And our top defense pair looked pretty weird going down the ice, one forward, one backward. But what about Alexia?

She was a great two-way player, an awesome checker, and an accurate passer. She had even cracked the top twenty in scoring. Last week I interviewed a kid from the Flames. He told me their coach spent half a practice working on how to play against Alexia. She *belonged* on the All-Star team! It wasn't fair!

Josh put an arm around his sister's shoulders. "Sorry, Lex."

She didn't say anything, but I could tell she was upset.

"Well, what do you know!" announced Happer Feldman right in our faces. "There aren't any space hicks on the All-Star team!"

"No, here's one!" exclaimed Oliver Witt. "Some jerk named Trent Ruben. He ran off and joined the Martians, remember?"

Last season, when Trent was a Penguin, he and those two creeps were known as the HOT line — *Happer, Oliver, Trent.* Now their center was a kid named Gavin, which made them the HOG line. Very fitting for pigs.

Happer turned his attention to Alexia. "Don't even bother looking for *your* name on there, *lady*," he sneered. "You think they're going to let a girl on the All-Star team?"

"Well, they should!" snapped Trent. "She's a better winger than either of you. This team is a joke if she's not on it!"

And Alexia did what I knew she was going to do, because she's not like anybody else in the world. Instead of being mad at Happer and Oliver, she blew up at Trent.

In a quiet voice that carried up and down the hall,

she said, "Who died and left you in charge of speaking up for me? Mind your own business!" And she stormed off, leaving Trent standing there with his mouth hanging open.

Oliver snickered. "Real classy team you're on now, Ruben."

Trent gave him a stony stare. "Like *you* would know anything about class."

We had to get out of there just to avoid a fight. I was still shaking my head as we walked away. "This is so wrong! There should be at least one Marser on the All-Stars."

Josh shrugged. "I guess our team started off so lousy — sure, we're better now. But our stats are nothing to brag about. You know — except for Lex."

"That's what I mean!" I persisted. "She should be on that list!"

Trent made a face. "Alexia could have more goals and assists than Wayne Gretzky and she wouldn't make that team. Not only is she a Marser, but she's also a girl. It's a double whammy."

"But don't you see how unfair that is?" I raved. "The All-Stars should be the best players, period! She's better than half those guys! King Diaper — big deal! She blows him away!"

"There's nothing we can do about it," Josh said sadly. "It's not our league. We just play in it."

Okay, I thought. Maybe Josh was right. The team couldn't do anything. It wasn't a player's job to expose unfairness and fight for justice. That responsibility belonged to someone who could sift through the garbage and get to the truth; someone who could bring that truth to the public; someone like — a reporter.

At times like these, it stinks to be a kid. If I worked for ESPN, I could just go on TV and tell everybody about this big rip-off. At *Sports Illustrated*, I could do a whole cover story on it. But the Waterloo Elementary School *Gazette* was a once-a-month paper. By the time the next issue came out, the All-Star tournament would be over!

I squared my shoulders and marched into Mrs. Spiro's class. "We need to publish a special emergency issue of the *Gazette*!"

She didn't even ask what for. She just said, "No."

"But —" I told her all that junk about the truth and the justice.

Mrs. Spiro, who was supposed to be a newspaper person, gave me this long lecture about the cost of paper. Paper! What could be cheaper than that? Even B.B. Balls, the smallest and chintziest jawbreakers, cost a dime. You could get a whole lot of paper for that ten cents.

The bell rang. And for the next hour, I had to pretend to be thinking about English. But I had something much more important on my mind. I had to figure out a way to bring this outrage to everyone's attention.

But how?

About the Author

When asked about his inspiration for *The Stars from Mars*, Gordon Korman says, "I started playing hockey when I was seven years old. I loved it, but I always ended up on teams with humiliating sponsors, like Stay Fresh Cleaning Service and Fish Buoy Restaurant. I remember one year we had a lot of bigger players, so we figured we could be the 'tough guys' of the league. Then we got our jerseys — Pretty Polly Paint and Wallpaper Inc."

Gordon Korman is one of Canada's best-loved authors for young people. He has more than fifty books to his credit, including *Born to Rock*, *Maxx Comedy* and the On the Run, Island, Everest, Dive and Macdonald Hall series. He and his wife, a teacher, currently live in New York with their three children.